The

Shaver Mystery Magazine
Vol 3 No 1 1949

Richard S. Shaver
Alfred Steber (Editor)

SAUCERIAN PUBLISHER
Original Sources in Ufology

ISBN: 978-1-955087-54-4

9 781955 087544

2023, Saucerian Publisher

PROLOGUE

Returning to the classics in any genre is generally a good idea. This also goes for UFO literature. Rereading a book or reviewing old documents after ten or twenty years is a rewarding experience. You will discover new data and ideas you didn't notice before. The reason, of course, is that you are, in many ways, not the same person reading the book the second or third time. Hopefully, you have advanced in knowledge, experience, and intellectual and spiritual discernment. A good starting point is to reread the UFO classics to understand the more profound mystery of what happened during that era.

This title is scarce and hard to find these days. The Shaver Mystery Magazine originally was published by the Shaver Mystery Club. This newsletter published the first printed stories on UFOs and was a major forum for debates about the occult, Forteans, and Lemurians. As Ray Palmer promoted it: "dedicated to the further study of the hidden truths as presented in the fact-fiction stories by Richard S. Shaver..."

In essence, the Shaver Mystery is a collection of stories in which Shaver claimed to have discovered proof of an evil humanity in underground caverns. Shaver portrayed an alien race that resided in Earth's caverns before escaping, leaving behind two distinct populations of offspring: the "Teros," a benevolent group of humanoids, and the "Deros," or "detrimental robots," a vile race who tormented and devoured humans. The Deros were especially brutal to women. The tales encouraged the establishment of Shaver Mystery Clubs.

The present edition is an authentic reproduction of the original Shaver Mystery Magazine printed text in shades of gray. **IMPORTANT,even though we have attempted to maintain the integrity of the original work, the present facsimile reproduction may have missing letters and blurred pages, poor pictures due to the age of the original scanned copy.** This magazine has been formatted from its original version for publication. Great, but unpretentious, this issue is an extraordinarily rare symbol of what was going on in those early years of the modern UFO phenomena.

Editor
Saucerian Publisher, 2023

SMALL HINDU TEMPLE

CONTENTS

Volume 3   1949   No. 1

THE SHAVER MYSTERY MAGAZINE

is Published by

THE ALDEBARAN PRESS

BOX 158, McHENRY, ILLINOIS

KEEP A TELAUG LOG

By: Vaag Tor

In view of the controversial aspects of the subject treated in this article, I must take the precaution of using a pen name, as long as a majority of people are still ignorant of the true nature of "voices in the head". As long as it is paradoxically lawful for a person to call the nut wagon for the innocent sane, I must protect myself from such a dangerous informant, who may have joined the Shaver Mystery Club (for all I know) merely for the purpose of spying on us --- as if we are living in a police state! That educated ignorance, that "know-it-all" attitude of people who are so handy with that "crackpot" label, is just what must have caused the Dark Ages. It is keeping rival atomic theories from obtaining a hearing and from seeing the light of day. It is what is keeping the psychiatric profession from becoming scientifically curious about what the "voices" say.

What is a "voice"? It is a telepathic signal received in the auditory center of the brain without the participation of the auditory nerves of the ear. Those who accept this explanation will naturally accept also the possibility of a source of such signals. Are the signals (or intelligences) exclusively from rays (1) beamed at us by telaug machines of the palatial catacombs, or do the messages come from disembodied spirits also? We should not discount any of the various theories merely because of concepts which we presume that they might contain, if we are scientific. We should rather tolerate with an open mind any theory that is awaiting experimental corroboration.

(1) For the benefit of those who have encounted oral or written arguments on scientific grounds why a penetray or a telaug beam could not possibly traverse many miles of solid rock, I have the following cogent data:

Shaver's critics are thinking of ether-waves which are wholly transverse in displacement. The presumptions that light consists only of transverse waves, and that the all-pervading ether must be an elastic solid for this reason --- (whereas the planets encounter negligible resistance in their obits) --- are the thought-tamper goads which caused the all-pervading either to become officially abolished.

1

So many members have asked for pictures of Shaver, that Dottie insisted I put this one in SMM to save wear and tear on the postman and and on her photo man at the drug store. So here it finally is for you. The one with the longest hair is Dottie. How it will look after going through our distinctly hazardous printing process, I wonder...

However, in 1906 Dr. Hermann Fricke, Ph.D., then the chief scientific adviser of the Kaiser' government, had announced his discovery that sound waves in air can have a transverse component, in addition to the usual longitudinal component. This led him to the idea that light probably has both kinds of component also, and that the ether therefore does not have to be a solid, but may be a kinetic gas as Huyghens (1629-1695) had supposed. In a lecture at Wolfenbuttel in 1909, "Uber die innere Reibung des Lichtathers als Ursache der magnestischen Erscheinungen", Dr. Fricke presented the ether as a gas with "inner friction". But at Konigsberg in 1910, Planck (discoverer of the energy quantum) delivered a lecture, attacking the new ether theory in mild, authoritative style. The ether, being thought "old-fashioned", was then officially "banished".

Nevertheless, in 1914 Fricke made a further discovery which rendered his ether concept still more valid in its new form. The new theory led to a solution of most of the cosmic problems and is still the basis of solutions of many other enigmas of Nature. But since the ether was "legally murdered", official science today remains deaf and blind to the great strides which the revised ether theories have made.

The experiments of R. Wussow ("Mechanik der Atherwellen unter Berucksichtigung der Transversalschwingungen", NATUR, Oct. 2, 1925, pp. 40-45) prove that longitudinal waves can develop a transverse component through suitable gratings or lattices under proper conditions. Indeed, this may be all that the transverse waves of light really amount to, the ether-waves being longitudinal and transverse at the same time. This evidence corroborates Dr. Fricke, but I believe that it also corroborates R. S. Shaver's findings about rays that penetrate many miles of solid rock, and without invoking meson-structure of such rock. It must be the longitudinal component of wave energy which is so penetrative.

Such component will not affect matter that is out of resonance with it, however; it is mostly the reansverse component which influences chemical changes, etc., as in a photographic film. (There may be anomalous cases; such as X-rays, whose transverse-wave displacements are so related to the wave length as to be able to go through a body and then register photographically.) Radio waves and sound waves can penetrate quite well, but because they are of the sine-wave type, they can be overcome also. But a saw-tooth wave would be a tough customer for opaque bodies to block.

This, and the following, are my opinions.

The advanced science behind the tealug machine design must have had thousands of prehistoric years of laboratory development. If the carrier-waves of longitudinal vibration employed in those machines have frequencies quite beyond the gamma-ray region, then interstellar communication via television would be theoretically possible with such waves travelling much faster than the speed of light. Any other frequency, especially the ultra-violet-like wave-bands used in a telaug beam, might then be in the nature of beat-frequency amplitude modulations. Such beams can transport mesons of amino-compounds for ben-ray purposes, thus acting like "pipes" or wave-guides, or can do many other marvelous things, such as read the pages of a closed book many miles away. Such is the precision of such machines, calibrated in vernier fashion to handle very accurately the most ticklishly critical corrections, putting our surface-world gun-sights to shame. A narrow shaft of telaug waves probably disturbs air molecules, to produce the visible fluorescence which on rare occasions has been seen at night. The longitudinal component of the proper frequencies can be transformed partially into the transverse component, by a process analogous to X-ray polarization, thus giving rise to visible light.

If the waves were of the saw-tooth type, then they would not only be superbly penetrative, but might act like a beam of force. This is how "meson-ized" atoms and molecules could be transmitted over a tight beam, either as a ben-ray delivering amino-radicals, or as a dis-ray delivering harsh frequencies of waves or radioactive atoms with bloated fields. However, the ability of a saw-tooth compressional wave to push anything, will depend on its frequency, which would have to be optimum --- just as the frequency of gentle taps must be optimum in order to push a large pendulum. It is quite possible that this principle was adapted in a certain way for use in the levitators, which hold space ships aloft.)

Vaag Tor

Those of my readers for whom disembodied spirits figure importantly in clairvoyant phenomena --- which need not involve the trance --- would be interested in ever-increasing fruitfulness of safe psychic technique, such as has been set forth in these works: (1) The Betty Book, and (2) a chapter on "Psychic Development" in J. Howard Cashmere's "Lost in the Bottomless Pit", the Merchants

Publishing Co., Denver, Colorado, 1905. An interesting specu-
lation of mine is that the pre-Adamic Elder race had not possessed
the higher faculties in their brains, such as we have (and neglect), and that the Elder mech was probably designed to serve as
a substitue.

Spirit phenomena may, after all, become de-occultized systems
which will readily lend themselves to correlation with the physical sciences. This will be possible when trained philosophers
coordinate all ambiguous terminology under valid, workable concepts, until a consistent, intelligible, scientific terminology
can be developed for use in a more scientific study of these
phenomena. Here is a rather intriguing concept: Man is really a
spirit-being clothed in a soul-body, which inhabits the control
room of a giant robot, which in turn exists on some sub-harmonic
plane of physical reality. Is a spirit simply a set of cavity-
resonators? Is the soul-body an aggregation of tiny "radio-
stations " (soul-cells) composed of mesons? These are questions
worth considering, but they are beyond the scope of our present
state of scientific knowledge. If the latter question be answered
in the affirmative, then it is conceivable why even the purest of
human sould must have rejuvenating transfusions from the Divine
IHVH, until a more perfect robot-body can be created to house it.
It is therefore the intention of the Beginning less One to popu-
late the Cosmos with superior creatures who will be immune to DE-
forces of any type. (Does the agnostic know a better method for
accomplishing this marvelous objective? Let's hear about it.
But study Job 38 esoterically first.)

So much for technical preliminaries. Now I shall outline a research procedure for the Club members to test, discuss, and ad-
vance.

In the dark, when notes are written down on what is heard tele-
pathically, some method should be followed to avoid large blank
spaces on the pad and much illegible overlapping of lines here
and there among the notes. By trial-and-error ways of taking
notes, I found that a cardboard guide with a slot in it along the
top edge, would be needed, to keep the lines straight when they
are written in the dark. Regularly spaced notches cut in the
edge of the guiding card provide little edges which can be trued
up with the edge of the pad, and this will facilitaxe the regu-
lar spacing of the lines. I alternate between a red-lead pencil

and a blue-lead pencil, both of them sharp of course: First a
blue line of notes, then a red line, then a line of printing with
the blue pencil, and so on. This will render legible both of the
two lines that have inadvertently been made to overlap each other.
Moreover, I do not use ordinary handwriting, but an alphabet of
curved letters with which the crossing of f's, t's and x's is
possible without losing the place. Instead of spaces between
sentences or unfinished signals, I use two vertical bars (like
those on a music staff.) This double bar indicates an indefinite
lapse of time between signals, which may be anythings from a few
seconds to several hours; or it might mean an intervening dream
or two, if a "D" follows the bars. Or, the reader may use his or
her own code of symbols.

Right after each telepathic-signal entry I sometimes mark down
certain symbols, which indicate signal intensity, voice quality
and sex, and even a cavern echo if I should happen to pick up one
in the signal. The intensity of the signal may depend not only
on the distance from the ray source, and on the cross-sectional
area covered by the telaug beam, but also on the state of reverie
of the conscious mind, whose degree of awareness may interfere
with sensitivity to the incoming signal.

Have you at times dreamed in the morning of listening to a radio
or of hearing a stentorian voice from the sky, which died away
into silence even as you pondered what was said? Did it have
telephone-like quality? That was telaug, my friend. Someone
down there tried to contact you. Either that, or you happened
to be listening in on one of the entertainment programs of an
interplanetary network, perhaps. Or else it might have been a
kind of "bait" to see whether or not you believe in the Shaver
Mystery.

Not all people have the same kind or degree of receptivity.
Some people, like myself, have developed mostly their clairaudient
faculty. Others receive visual signals best. A failure to understand the underlying phenomena has in past centuries been the
cause of many peculiar sects and "isms", but we must take care
not to lump all religion under this heading. I have seen two
flash visions which I ascribe to telaug, for want of a religious
significance. One time at night I saw for a couple seconds a
ravishingly beautiful girl with brown curly hair, dark eyes, and
a brown velvet dress to match, with arms of a lighter color.
She looked up askance from a book on her lap, smiled, and golden-
ly intoned: "Pulling so quick?" At later date I saw before me
a wrinkled scientist in a white tunic, who told me with a trance
of displeasure in his look: "It will help to make athe circuit. "
(He may have meant that my dozing in semi-consciousness or
reverie, wo,ld increase my receptivity for better signals.) If
you have little or no auditory receptivity, then you might try
to improve on it by imagining at dusk that you are listening to
a gurgling brook. This should bring results, if you keep it up.
The room need not be so dark, but there must be silence. If you
live in a noisy neighborhood (not counting the trains in), then
the middle of the night is the best time. If the light intensity is the same to you whether the eye-lids are open or shut, you
can test yourself for visual receptivity. Don't count on the
cavern aristocracy being very cooperative, however.

For ferreting out information on the subterranean conditions
that exist behind the deros' "iron curtain" hung from pole to
pole and from the Greenwich Line to Longitude 360 degrees, there
seems to be no reliable wya to obtain the correct context f bm a
series of unrelated notes. I get phrases or fragments of sentences, but I write them down just as they come to me, and I
conclude that these are segments of thought from beams that whip

5

past me like a search-light scanning pleasure row-boats at night. If I pick up some very rapidly spoken (or thought) phrasds, then I conclude that a Doppler Effect is involved where the focus of a talaug beam ascends toward me. It is difficult to learn much from mere signals alone, but if a cavern-dweller would risk kindling the rage of the dero rulers by shielding his telaug beam with a cylindrical shorter-ray barrier -- which cannot go unnoticed on a visi-screen but which is always taken to mean that secrets are being beamed up to the surface -- then a great deal of information could be learned from him, but not for very long. Thus far there has been no shorter-ray channel for me, and therefore my knowledge of the caves and stim-beams is very limited. I made an attempt, however, to get some sense out of all my notes on telepathic signals, by arranging strips of paper in columns. The best result obtained so far is the following:

"A drip on aritmetic. He write down. Contact him. "
"Whatcher name? Why don't you sit? "
"Provide his features. Vote sacrifice. Com here! Come. Find. "
"Cycle ration jar. Isn't nicked. Go and get it; they might destroy it. "

The above sample may interest the Cave Hunters' Mutual Benefit Society, but on the other hand, there is practically no clue there to go on. But many of the telepathic signals I have received since September 1947 do not have great proof value for the Shaver Mystery. Here they are, taken at random:

"Short --- terrible --- dero --- bent "
"Paved experiences. "
"Two hearts depending on her sub-technical will. "
"Clamped censorship. "
"Crime table. "
"Put on your harness. "
"Ben 16 "

"--- where the Moon silences. "
"Solya, -- " (A regal-sounding voice of a lady, with cavern echo blended in.)
"Medical trail. "
"Rope the temple. "

The original notes, dated like a diary and kept unaltered in any way, have considerable proof value, especially if they contain slang or jargen which is peculiar to the cavern world and which is found also in the notes of other Club members. In case the Shavery Mystery should ever go on trial in a chancery court, then the validity of all claims will be examined in observance of the Laws of Evidence, and the "telaug logs" of the Club members, if then available in undestroyed quantity, would have much testimonial value -- especially if tall sessions of the jury could be screened off by shorter-ray barries so that "thought-tamper" would not influence their decision. I would urge as mnny Club members as possible, herein, to keep a telaug log. (Do not disclose to your relatives or friends the fact that you are doing this, unless they first volunteer to you the information that they believe in the existence of Shaver's caves and their telaug mech.)

There is one note of caution that I wish to trumpet at this point, however. That is that you must make sure of the general area in which you live, as to what sort of beings inhabit the caverns beneath you. Do strange crimes occur frequently in your county? If so, then do not risk sending a thought back along a telaug beam when it sweeps your way. The dero are probably down there. And they are unequalled in the viciousness of their practical "jokes". On the other hand, if all signs seem to show that friendly ray-people are down there, then listen eagerly, but do not

reply with a strong thought unless they ask you who you are, etc.,
in which case they are not rude enought to probe the inner con-
fidences of your life or whatever you have that you never broad-
cast. Go about it as a cautious agent of the military G-2 would
do.

There is a great deal of fun in collating telaug notes, for a
little while, until you come to a startling realization that this
is no fun at all for the slaves and puppet aristocrates down below.
To record as many hundreds of signals as I have at night, and to
read these notes indiscriminately after sundown, is an almost sure
way to become guilty of innocent blood. I do not know what happened down there after I started this strange hobby; perhaps the
slaves were only repremanded or lashed for alleged espionage for
which they were not responsible. I HOPE they were not tortured
for confessions. Who knows how many people or how many secrets
were involved? Do not do as I did: Reading a Telaug Log during
twilight hours. The telaug beams are reconnoitering surface-world
thoughts during such hours, when the sunlight is not present to
irritate their bodies. They are especially keeping watch over all
Shaver Mystery fans. And I know from what I picked up in the night
that I was one to be feared, for I was careless -- at first.

The best way to keep Telaug Logs is to prepare them at night and
tuck them away somewhere without reading them, except perhaps in
the bright sunlight where only the most insane dero would brave
the DE-streams to eavesdrop on your thoughts. Keep the logbooks
you prepare in a safe place, for you may need them at some future
date.

For the languishing troll-fodder of the palatial catacombs, WAR
time seems NEVER to come to an end. The scattered rebel-bands
who are friendly to us surface-dwellers but have great difficulty
in getting us to listen to them, are busy fighting for their lives,
and for ours also. Here is our chance to give them the help which
for centuries has been denied them by that "educated ignorance"
of our world; we can produce 'Telaug Logbooks" in great numbers
for purposes of satisfying the demands of the Laws of Evidence.
Only in this way can we start a peoples' movement of gretx momen-
tum, which eventually can overcome all dero opposition by sheer
weight of numerical superiority. A LITTLE LEAVEN LEAVENETH THE
WHOLE LUMP. Just so, a little PROOF can lead to more research on
the part of many, and that in turn will lead to still MORE proof,
and so on, until officially tolerated, recognized, and assisted
clubs and drives can begin to take action --- for humanity's
SURVIVAL. Must we wait until the day that the dero foist a
counterfeit 'Messiah" on the panic-stricken world??

Hummm --- Wow! What's your 'set" picking up lately?

Sample notes of voices heard by me to compare - Shaver.

'Make a bad report by the night.... "
(means they have a monitor who makes marks after names of
each that transgresses the multiplicity of rules. A realy
bad mark means whipped - and a whipping means infection,
frequetnly death, for there is no sun and disease and infection are prevalent.)

'Want" - sort of chorus effect to impress upon one the true
atmosphere. "

'Disease"

'Without a doubt the most horrible" (tamper shorter here cuts off the rest of this sentence - the tamperer is a regenerate stool who is himself in misery from neglect ...)

'No medecine"

"Important boss idiot mind"

"Swing over a pit of coals by your arms, if you relax, pain makes you start swinging again until at last weakness forces you to let the high flames zt the center devour your flesh.)

'Egging a walkin" Walking around bed coals" (favorite pastime of ray-rule for punishment is to make person walk into coals by ray control to mind until legs are at last burnt off short - still the stumps can be made to move even after dealth. "

'Eggin" means suggesting it to sadist ruler..."

'These people are from your cities, I am too - Police are afraid to open their mouths.

'Thick" - (means minds of old families of caves are affected by life there till stupid)

'Flay" -- chorus

"it's everything - " trying to impress me with the importance of cavern world and life upon our own surface world - it is everything, our trouble and our pain and our worst enemy - as well as our best possible chance of pulling out of this".

'Get a cab" is a threat, and is true, for one way to get into caves inadvertently is to take a cab the driver of which is paid to bring victims to caves, where they are speedily impressed into slaver and work hard to escape beatings, which are fatal too often.

'We've getting sick! Is there help? (across) Have you a government? "(He is getting over the usual mental state of those imprisoned and enslaved in the caves from surface life who cannot realize their life-long impression of a beneficient surface government being supreme is false, and they have no hope of government interference...")

Fosts - Comparise - Sheet

(Examination sheet of youngster on test of knowledge of how deinfection hereditary character deformation is seen in the young.)

Morose - (child is morose - same meaning as our word)

Uses disparaging sound in play laugh - Oh-he -

Yeah * says yes meaning no - usual reversal of normal meaning found in dero thought - our 'Oh yearh"

Placedhere - remains in assigned position when a normal child p
Placidear - does not when dero - placedhere is usual shortened
Place adhere word form of edder tongue - for place adhere - used combined words in this way also meant "placid dear" and "play see dee heref" (ability to tell de in others) (a sea lawyer in play - who objects to dirty play without rules)

Reminds me - test for good child - tell to remind teached of something and he does - dero does not.

Weticos - we-tic-owes - one who owes always to the energy bank or
          state credit system - they had refined this meaning to
          embrace a general concept of cooperation - a wetico was
          one who owed energy to the general pool of man-energy -
          a bad child was easily distinquished by these used to
          watching for "leaners" "clinging vines" etc.

A good child is good to his pets and other pet animals - a bad
child always cruel -

Youinblame - chile alwyas blames others for his shortcomings - dero

Flossjerkin - nervous fingered - like plucking of a dying person at
             covers -

Scandarprompt - was the word for an expert monitor of this system
               of picking out the bad eggs from the school child-
               ren and advising treatment.

So that you may glimpse the workings of the minds of this giant
people - I give yoo this sheet - a part of their system of screen-
ing out derrish youngsters from their races children. The youngsters failing these tests were exiled to "derrish" planets.

ELDER POEM

I sing myself   I sing myself
in all my variation   from all my pasts
in all my times   into all my futures
in all my beings   I come - singing
I sing me   I go - a song
I am man: I am man
One thing   One thing
Man   Only
And no other   Man-tree
Only   Me:
Man-tree:

The meaning in English of an Elder poem.

WATCHER

That night I sat with Her, during her turn at watch - and she
spoke of the old things that were known, such as:

"somewhere, far off in space, there is still the Tree. You see,
tree isn't just a tree, to them it meant the symbol of many
branches - their own race and all its relatives back and back
from many places in space where the ancestors came from. It meant
a lot more than that, too.

Ygdrasil meant the life - tree, a thought, a memory of the time
when the sap of life flowed unquenched, renewing man's strength
against all demands, making him and his woman and his people
greater always.

The Nidhogg gnawed the root, and that Nidhog has us of the tree
in his grip today. Most of us do not know that there really is
a tree called "Yg." Ygdrasil was the immortal, ever-growing
bracnhsx of the tree of life itself, intelligent ever-growing
life, god-like in its power of renewal and eternal strength."

9

It was in this vein she spoke, and I listened. To me, then, she typified everything of which she spoke, so lucidly, unknowing in her wise eyes was the answer to the question she propounded - at least for me.

She spoke of a man she had known, of us, the people of today: 'The bright beginnings of the man, the fierce wild job of life within him. Then, to see it crushed, in the degrading dirt of scandal and disease and utter corrupt idiocy of that thing that did crush him - it was more than one could bear.

Then when it came time to mate, there was no hold, no wy, no answer to the mess - so he fell.

But hasn't the whole race lost the best fruit from the tree always? Isn't it a gloomy fate staring man in the face, out of the past might-have-beens?

How many bright beginnings blighted, and all to do again. Too, too many. Yet still Ygdrasil puts out new shoots, and brave heros trudge out and battle for the right sort of lifeway for the sons of Yg, and no life-way comes of it, but only the endless warring and the misery and waste of good life stock.

Where would the life-shoot grow to, if it were not always thus blighted? What is the purpose that Ygdrasil strives for, what infinite bright purpose does the life-tree grow toward? What is life itself about, and what is it that thwarts it, and if it were not thwarted -- where would it grow?

If one could picture the really great fulfillment of all these bright beginnings? If one could know the ultimate answer to it all that the great old life of Ygdrasil knows and tries to bring into reality about us, would one not help more, not try harder?"

And she was herself one bright fulfillment - the answer to her question, the ultimate promise and the goal of all the growth. She was the dream before the heroes eyes as he wore off his feet marching to make the dream come true.

Unknowing what she was, she pondered thus why all the life-effort toward what goal. She was the drama of the play, the heroine, the brave but undefeated mother... She was the blood and the seed of Yg, pondering how to grow into the life-tree she was meant to be.

And she was dying, there in the dark at her work. Dying, and yet trying to yet one more time make the dream of herself come true for some other -- some other less able and less worthy - but then she was unable to get out of the prisoning. And once out, unable to use the power that tonight was hers at the watch-post.

'So there you were, and the night above, so unlike the night here below -- with its stars, and its moon and its leaf scented air and brisk, pleasant breeze. "

So explaining, her ray went on its way, and left me.

. . . .

Watch rays guard the ray-groups always, listening with long range telaug reaching for many miles, and hearing a medley of all mens thought and all the sounds that all those men hear so that they can pick out danger from afar and focus a beam upon it. So listening to the generalized thought of so many minds mingling - they know life - and are more than other minds not so employed.

Such was my meeting with one, and the man she explained whom she had watched grow into his "bright beginning" and then become enmeshed in scandal and crushed by disease - by the thing against which she guarded her own ray-people - the rods who torment and control and destroy so many of us surface people with the ancient rays. She had seen so many, so much of the mental life of all men in the city over her rays, seen inside their minds en masse, knowing all men and all women as no other kind of woman ever knows them. These are the people who are the hope of the future, and they fail, the world will continue on its dark, repetitive path of futile effort toward a goal that is - delusion. We must find a way to serve, a way to bring about that fulfillment.

You see, there is no slightest accident in our cities that does not immediately get a look-see from a watch ray from below - who heard the mental uproar from afar with her augmenting mech - and swings a beam instantly to focus. You wonder how many - but it does not matter. The tools they use multiply their efficacy until they seem not to need the numbers we count necessary for strength. Besides, many are our friends, a part of us by long knowledge of our ways and out thoughts, and only the evil rods are really our enemies among the ray people.

They have always done us small favors, and one day they will do us the big one, mingling that science they inherit with our own, and man will set foot on the stair to the stars --

But let us hear no more of the usual "occult" wool - "we are not ready for that wisdom."

We are as ready as they, after the history they have to show for their opportunities. We are as much a part of them as themselves, and they of us. They know us from the indide, not like our surface friends, from the surface of the face only. They know us from reading our minds daily and nightly, as they must do inadvertently listening over the telaugs for danger approaching along the cavern ways, or swooping down the paths of space from -- where Do disc ships come from?

Man has only one enemy, the rod or dero, the naturally evil mind. Most of the sane ray people know this, it was the most common teaching of the Elder race, and they have learned it. When man learns to sieve out his deros from among his children, exiling them before they come to the age of destructive ability and power -- when man learns to keep his "tree" clean of the rotten fruit -- evil will pass away and we will begin to progress.

But let us not hear again, "men are not ready for the wisdom or the weapons of the caversn." They are quite as ready and more so than those evil wights who incessantly mutilate our life with their work, unseen by us.

"WE THE TERO, SPEAK!"

4-4 (Myia): 'There are places where we can get up if we really want something from up there badly enough, but we don't like to do it. We feel defenseless and insedure, and get sick if we stay too long. Be kind to the Gypsy fortune tellers you meet. Some of them might be us. That's the favorite disguise. We don't come

up often. It costs so much to get out, and they rob us blind
coming back in. Often they demand the very things we wanted the
most. I've never been up. When some go up, others must stay down
to cover them, and that's always been my job."

"What does steak taste like? I've heard so many people thinking
about it, and it seems good. Is it really?"

"Wish I had a radio, but don't dare. They radiate too much. Think
some of the latest songs for me. I can hear them that way."

4-5 (Myia): "The reason so many science-fiction stories sound so
real is because they are real. That's one way of trying to tell
you people something. We seldom actually tell you anything, just
put out hints. If anyone is bright enough to get it, all well and
good. If not, to Hell with it. They don't deserve to know. They
beam these things to the stf. writers because they're about the
only ones whose minds will entertain the ideas. The scientists
and professors are too 'intelligent' to believe that sort of
stuff! "

"Yes, I know all about the professors you're thinking about. They
aren't as bad as some, but those weren't their ideas. Some one
put them into their heads. Guess who?"

"Most of your scientists and political leaders are wormy. Certainly
we use that expression down here. Why shouldn't we? It came from
here. A lot of the slang and expressions you use came from here.
They weren't thought up just for amusement. They mean something.
Someone's trying to tell you something. Study the teen age slang
and jive talk. A lot of it is beamed to them because they'll
pick it up and spread it around. If it gets spread around enough,
maybe someone will figure out what it means. Only they never do.
Study a few of them. Don't be a z-ro all your life!"

"Wormy? Why, because they are wormy. They have worms in their
brain. When they try to think, only part of the tought channels
get thru. The others are obstructed by worms. So their ideas
are screwy. There's another one for you to figure out. Your
scientists have electron microscopes up there. They could see
them, if they'd only take the trouble to look! But their books
don't tell them that!"

4-7 (Ira): "Sometime try to figure out why a compass varies all
over the map. Ask some of your professors. They'll tell you it's
caused by metal deposits. Then ask them why it changes, and see
what they say. Do the metal deposits move around? You never
heard that the earth generates power, like a huge dynamo, did you?
Not knowing that, you naturally wouldn't know what effect it would
have if someone tapped off some of that power for some purpose,
say to run some huge ray mech. On second thought, maybe it's just
as well you don't know. If you did, you could take a map of magnetic declinations and sit down and figure out where it was being
tapped off, and that might be very unhealthy!"

4-8 (Myia): "Sometimes someone will try to get an idea across by
beaming it to a song writer, but it seldom works. Did you ever
hear a basso solo: 'Murder in the Moonlight?' If you had ever
scanned some of the horrible affairs some of the things down here
hold, you'd know what the song meant. It was written as a sola
because when these things get their hands on you, you're all alone.
No one can help you then. It's a basso solo because basso is low
- 'way down deep. 'Murder' because that's the least you can call
these affairs. 'Moonlight', because they usually hold them when
the moon is high. It helps stim them to that sort of thing."

'"Loony'. Ever wonder about that? When a person is under the influence of Luna, they're luny. People are so dumb they don't even spell it right! Ask the nurses at any insane asylum when they have the most trouble with their patients. They know!"

'Why does a dog howl at the moon? Figure that out and you'll be a lot wiser than you are now. It can sense something. Humans can't sense it, but it affects them. Think it over. What senses does a dog have that people don't have? You could make instruments to detect it, but people probably wouldn't believe it even if you did. The people who believe that a howling dog is a sign of dealth aren't just following a silly superstition. They have part of the answer. The same thing that makes the dog howl is likely to result in sudden death. There's another subject for you to study: Superstitions. A lot of them are based on some fact, even if they don't have their facts straight."

4-12 (Myia): "You hear a lot of interesting gossip down here. Like the one about Roosevelt not being dead. I don't know anything for sure, just heard the rumor. The way it goes, a group down here had been working on his to change the atomic bomb project into a peacetime atomic power project. They finally got him convinced, and was ready to issue the necessary orders. The munitions, coal and power gang knew what was happening. They all have rays down here."

'None of them like it. They were getting a juicy cut out of the bomb development, and they knew it would be cut down if it was switched to power. The sky was the limit for war weapons, but he wouldn't dare spend that much for peacetime uses. Also, it would destroy the value of their coal and power holdings. They figured they had to stop him. They didn't want to kill him. They thought it would be smarter to blast his brain into complete imbicility. Then they could say he had been mentally off all along, and it would be easier to get Congress to repeal a lot of laws they didn't like."

'What they wanted done is a very delicate job, and takes a lot of skill. No one here who could do it would do it. So they got a hood from Europe to do the job. They'd imported him several months before for just such an emergency. He did a good job. Several friendly rays examined his brain at once and saw that it was hopeless. Nothing they had would repair the damage. Maybe there's mech here that could do it, but no one knows where it is, or how to run it."

'The frinedly rays spoiled the second part of the plan. They got to Mrs. Roosevelt and some key government men at once and convinced them to report him dead. He was secretly taken to an isolation ward, and the funeral held over a weighted casket. Did you ever know that, except for the doctors and possibly the family, no one actually saw him after the report of his death? The casket was never opened. Mrs. Roosevelt wouldn't even permit it to be opened for some close friends."

'Do you remember what Mrs. Roosevelt said when she was told of his death? 'I feel sorrier for the people of the United States, and of the world, than for us.' Friendly rays had already told her what had been done, who had done it, and why. She knew what the score was, and she felt sorry for the people. She knew that there was a group so powerful and ruthless that they'd even destroy a president who got in their way. She had reason to feel sorry for you. Read your old papers since that time. Every one in the government that the coal and power gang didn't like has been quietly eased out of the government. Every law they didn't like has been quietyly 'amended' so that it can't work. All limits have been taken off

13

their profits. Who got the income tax cuts? Maybe you got a few
cents cut tossed to you, but who got the folding money cuts?
Truman knows what they can and will do. Ever notice how suddenly
he reverses himself at times? Orders! "

'I talked to a ray who usually works under Washington. He tried
to check the rumor, but had to break contact before he found anything very definate. Things are really rugged under Washington.
Thirty or forty different rod and goon squads, all working for
someone. Your friends and allies today may be your worst enemies
tomorrow. You have to keep up to date on your 'who's who' if you
want to stay alive there. Some rays seem to like that sort of
life. Personally, I wouldn't even go near the place. You'd
better keep all this about Roosevelt to yourself. Your government
would toss you into stir and throw the key away before you could
tell a dozen people, if some rod didn't get you first. I don't
really know anything about it, just heard it. "

4-15 (Myia): 'No, I don't know Shaver personally. I've heard
of him from people who have come thru from there, and I've read
most of what he's written. We're interested in anything of that
sort. Sometimes we get the actual books and magazines in various
ways, and sometimes we get it out of some fan's head. Recently,
I've been reading it the same time you did; out of your head!
Didn't know you had company right there inside your brain, did
you? Better be careful what you think. No matter what youre
thinking, Myis know it! And you ought to be ashamed of yourself
sometimes! Or, should you? "

'Shaver's stuff is mostly right. He's doing a good job, and has
a lot of friends here. There are a few things different from the
way we have them, but maybe he's rught. There's a lot of ids-
agreement between tapes sometimes. Maybe his are right, maybe
ours are. Who knows? Few of the tapes you find here were actually
made by the gods. Those who made them were much later, and didn't
always seem to know what they were talking about. Lots of times
they were just thinking out what they'd heard, of what they had
personally figured out. Maybe they had it right, maybe they didn't.
Who can say for sure? "

'My father used to be the real expert on the tapes. He'd spend
all his spare time with them, and run them over and over until he
was sure he had the exact shade of meaning. Then he'd hold regu-
lar classes for all us kids. He made all the kids in the family
go to your schools too. Get a class on the beam and make us study
the lessons right with the kids in the class. He's not here now.
About two years ago, under South Carolina, he met a papa-lou who
had wandered over from Africa, and the papa-lou saw him first.
My uncle killed the papa-lou, but it was too late to do dad any
good. "

(Note: 'papa-lou' is the phonetic spelling. It may not be the
correct way to spell it. I never heard the word before, and contact was cut before I could find out exactly what it was. Apparently some sort of 'undesirable'.)

4-19 (Myia): 'We've had tapes similar to Shaver's 'Mandark".
In ours, 'Yahveh' had a different name, but it's the same incident.
His story isn't finished, of course, so don't know whether it
agrees with ours or not. In ours, Yahev and Christ were merely
the last of a series of 'experiments' to regenerate the human race.
Osiris, Moses, and Gautama Buddha had been sent here before them,
each with a different approach to the problem. Like a research
worker: If one experiment fails, he tries another one slightly
different. "

'The gods knew what was going on all time time, and could have stepped in and altered the situation at any time, but this would have ruined the value of the experiment. In order to find out what they wanted to know, they had to let it run to its own conclusion. When it had done this, they made their decision That the situation was hopeless. The human race could not be regenerated 'until the tides of de had ebbed.' The old fellow who made the tape quoted frome something 'The tides must run their natural course, must ebb and flow in their apponted times. Even the gods themselves can neither stay nor hasten them.' Yahveh and Crhist were restored by Elder surgery and medical mech, and taken to the home of the gods. They are still there, together with the other 'messengers' who had been sent before them, awaiting the time when they can return and rehabilitate what is then left of the race.''

4-21 (Myia): 'I've been going over some of dad's tapes, and found something else connected with 'Mandrake'. In one place, Shaver says that he believes that the Bible is only part of a much larger book, He's right. Dad found a tape made by some old fellow who apparently had made a life study of the subject. I don't know what the gods called this original record, but this man referred to it as 'The Seven Sacred and Inspired Writings, from that ancient Motherland of man which was where is now only the sea.''

'The original records were on metal plates, and several copies were deposited at different places in the caverns. There are rumors that they still exist, but no one knows where. Copies were later made of baked.clay, for use at various places on the surface. They made them by pressing the wet clay into the metal plates, thus giving a reversed impression. They used to ink these clay tablets and take a copy off on parchment. Who said printing was new? He didn't know all the places on the surface where these tablets were left, but they are supposed to still exist in Burma and Thibet, guarded by the priests in secret archives. They wouldn't let you see them. They're so 'holy' that you have to $belong to the lodge' to see them. You couldn't read them if you did see them. They're written in a special language, not used by the common Elders, and known only to the gods themselves. The priests who guard them can't even read them. If they ever had the key to the language, they've lost it. The old fellow who made the tape said: 'The gods neither entrusted their secrets and mysteries to everyone, nor degraded them by disclosing them to the profane. They were reserved for those who had proven themselves worthy of them.''

'Moses had the whol story. The gods taught him to read the tablets which were in the Egyptian temple archives. He copied them correctly and completely. It was those who came after him who did the dirty work. The Hebrew priests gradually forgot how to redd the Egyptian temple language which Moses had used so, about 800 years after the Exodos, Ezra and some others attempted to translate them into Hebrew. They didn't really understand the characters either, and made an awful mess of it. A lot was let out. Some of the most important scrolls seem to have been lost during their wanderings.''

'All the religions in the world are based on these same old writings. None have the complete story. All have been distorted by an ignorant and corrupt priesthood. This old fellow knew some of the ancient original writings, from old tapds and such. It was not just a religion. It was their history and science too. They believed in some sort of 'Primary Cause', but not as a personified 'Being'. I think I have their point of view, but it's difficult to explain. It was something you can't describe. You mind couldn't get the proper concept, because it was something entirely outside your experience. They called it 'The Unnamable'. They believed that the sould survived the death of the body, but not that it retained its individuality or personal memories. They used the word 'kui', instead of 'soul'. There is a difference, but I can't translate 'kui' so that you would understand it, so I said 'soul'. We still have some of his tapes. As soon as I have time, I'll run them over again to refresh my memory, and tell you the important parts."

4-28 Note: The following is from the old tapes mentioned above.)"

'These things we know:

This earth and sun, and all the countless worlds in space, and all therein and thereon, were created according to the desire and command of the Unnamable, but were actually created by the Sacred Four. (*) Therefore: They are mortal things. Each, in its appointed time, will perish, and go back to the elements from which it was created."

'The kui of man is directly of and from the Unnamable, and is a part of its immortal and eternal being. Therefore: It is imperishable and indestructable."

'Man does not come into being only cone, and then depart forever. He lives many times, in many places, but not always upon this earth. Between each life, there hangs a veil of darkness. He knows nothing of his past lives, except some fleeting thought carries him back to some circumstance of a previous existence. He does not recall the details, only that the person, place, or event is familiar. In time, the kui of man will reach its appointed perfection. The veil shall be rent, and the doors shall be opened, to show him all the chambers thru which he has wandered."

'The kui of man is eternal. Now eternity, having no ending, can have no beginning. It is a circle. Therefore, if this one thing must necessarily also be true, namely: That we have always lived."

'Life does not end with the death of the mortal body. Therefore: Love, being the vital force of life, must endure while life endures. The strength of this invisible power will bind two kuis together long after this world is dead. Death is but the nursemaid that puts the kui to sleep, nothing more. In the morning, it will wake again, to travel thru another day with those who have companioned it in all of its wanderings. It may not recognize its companions, but it will be drawn to them as ioon is drawn to the lodestone."

'You, yourself, are both Heaven and Hell. (*) Heaven is but the inner glow of contentment which will come with the perfection of the kui to complete understanding, to oneness with the Unnamable. Hell is the discontent, reproach and self-abasement which will come with the realization that the kui, by its own evil thought and deed, has strayed from the pathways to perfection; has degraded itself. The deeds of one life will carry forward to those which follow. even 'tho they be not remembered. If they be good, they will enrich and beautify the kui in the lives to come. If they be evil, they will degrade the kui, and trouble it, until they have been attoned. It is not needful that I should relate to you the laws, nor chart for you the pathways. Your secret inner selves, your own kuis, know that which is good and that which is evil, that which is te and that which is de."

'These things we know."

'You who come after us, have faith to believe."

'It has been said"

(Note:* The 'Sacred Four' do not seem to have been divinities. They appear to have been a group of super-gods, far superior to the ordinary Elder gods. Among other things, they are said to have

16

the power to create by mental means alone, altho they usually augmented this power with mech. They created man's body 'after their own fashion'. The Unnamable added his kui after its own fashion. The words 'heaven' and 'hell' are used because the old Elder words used by the maker of the ancient tape have no exact equivalent in modern language. They are similar in meaning, but not exactly the same.)

5-1 (Myia): "J'Yesm we have no bananas' came from down here. It wasn't a message to you people. It was sort of a 'newscast' for us. People up there would circulate it around, and people down here who had no direct contact with each other would hear it and get the news. It was about a move to capture some entrances. People here knew the main crop grown near each one, so mentioning them was the same as naming the locality. They had no bananas because they couldn't get up to get them. Things hadn't gone so well down in banana country. They had these other vegetables, which meant that they could get up to get them, so they had captured those places. It didn't mean much very long. The new groups soon became as bad as the old ones had been, if not worse. Something like being 'liberated' by the Russians."

5-2 (Myia): Saw a couple of leprechauns the other day. They're cute! Awfully shy, 'tho. Guess the big folks give them a tough time. Don't know what they were doing this far from home. They seldom come here."

T-7 (Ira): 'Shaver's ideas on sun disintegration are correct so far as they go, but they don't go far enough. According to the tapes we have, which are supposed to have come from the original Elder plates, the de in our solar system comes from the combustion of the sun, but the nature of the sun's combustion, in turn, is caused by the nature of the etheric 'cloud' which we're in -- the 'tide of de'. You can heat metal very hot, in the proper atmosphere, and merely melt it, and make it give off light and heat. You can heat it to the same temperature in a different sort of atmosphere, and it will burn and give off noxious fumes. It's something the same with a sun. That's not the whole story, of course. It's not actually as simple as that. Some of the elements in the 'tide of de' itself are converted and radiated. What I've told you is the general idea. When the 'tide of de' leaves, the nature of the solar radiations will again change."

"The maximum height of de, the flood tide, as it were, is right about now, 1948, as nearly as we could translate the old dates. From now on, it will begin to lessen in intensity. The change is likely to be marked by a considerable increase in sun spot activity. When you cut down the draft on a roaring fire, it may spit and back fire for a while. All this doesn't mean that people can just sit back and let nature take its course. The tides run slowly. Thousands of years. Even after the de radiations stop, many of the effects will remain until someone corrects them. Those who know should work harder than ever. They'll be going with the flow of the tide now, instead of against it, so should have more success."

5-9 (Myia): "You see a lot of funny things down here. A couple of years ago we met a space traveler. He wouldn't say where he was from. Just 'A long way off' -- somewhere outside our solar system. A rod killed him. Funny thing, he looked human, but when the ray hit him, he mewed and spit like a cat! Before that, when I was barely old enough to remember, there were a group of spacemen from Mars here. Their ship was disabled in some way, and they destroyed it to keep it from falling into the earthmen's hands, so they came down here to wait for another ship which came tp get them. They had weapons to blast their way past the guards. They looked very much like us, except that they had three eyes, and a sort of orchid complexion. My father's cousin, Cyril, is a medicon, and examined some of them. He's here now, and I'll let him tell you about them."

(Cyril): "The third eye wasn't really an eye, as it had nothing to do with the sense of sight. It's a sense that most people on this planet have developed only partially, if at all: Telepathy and, possibly, clairvoyance -- altho I'm not certain about the latter. We have the same organ, but it's latent. The ancients knew of it. They called it the 'mind's eye', and the expression still remains, altho few people realize what it means. The old head binders tried to develope these senses by binding the heads of their children, thus putting pressure on the nerves of this rudimentary organ, and irritating it into action."

fiTheir complexion is artificial. They are naturally a light blond race, similar to the terrestrial nordics. These particular people were hereditary spacemen. The families had followed the profession for generations. When their children are about a year old, they drain out all their blood and replace it with a synthetic fluid. The reason is that, out in space, they are exposed to different radiations than on a planet, and some of these are much more harmful than any we know. They are all of the heavy metals group, of course, and ordinarily will settle in the bones and tissues. This synthetic blood, among other things, has the property of holding these products in suspension, so that they will not be deposited in the body. They remain in the fluid. It is this synthetic blood which gives them their peculiar complexion."

'Every so often they have their blood replaced with a new supply, which is free from radioactive poisons. It is compounded specially for each individual, according to his or her mineral requirements, and has the proper antibodies for all known germ diseases. You get a new set of vacinations and immunizations with each blood change! The old blood is cleansed of the radioactive poisons, mainly by centrifuging, and reprocessed for the next change. We couldn't learn the formula. That's one of their trade secrets. There are some physical differences too. Changes in the circulatory and eliminatory systems to make them function better in low or zero gravity. Some are surgically induced, but most of them are hereditary. Darwin's theory. Those who weren't physically suited for space conditions died young and didn't leave many children behind them. Thus, the group gradually changed. These people weren't native to Mars, altho they have lived there for many ages. They speak of other people there also, some quite different from themselves. They either didn't know, or wouldn't say, where their people originally came from."

5-14 (Myia): "A ray came thru from under-Washington recently with some more interesting gossip about the coal and power gang. He says that Lewis knows, but keeps his mouth shut, and will even play ball with them now and then, if they make it worth his while. They'd get him if they dared, but he has protection down here too. A rod and goon squad of his own. Neither side wants to start anything until they're sure they're able to finish it, and they're too evenly balanced. The two gangs are constantly fighting down here, but leave the big shots up there pretty much alone. Sort of an armed truce. Lewis's gang has taken a few beatings recently. Not decisive, but enough to let them get tougher with him on the surface, and to make him be more careful. Ever notice how he sometimes delays appearing at some hearing, or in court, even if it means a big fine? His gang needs the time to get in position to cover him. He's covered all the time. Ever notice how he will suddenly walk out on something, without any apparent reason? Something has happened. His gang either can't or won't stay where they can cover him any longer."

'This rumor is another thing you'd better not talk about. It

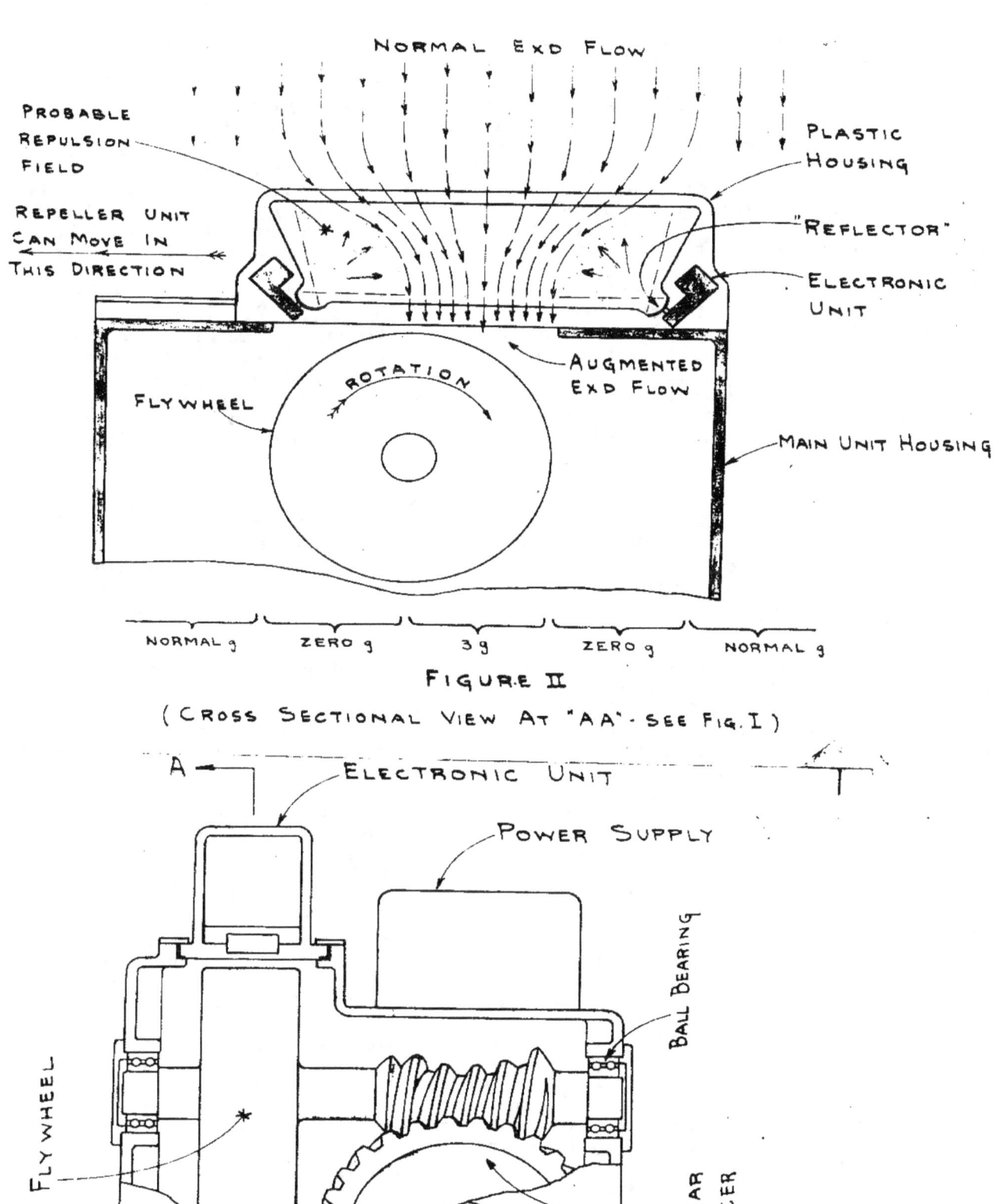

NORMAL EXD FLOW

PROBABLE REPULSION FIELD

REPELLER UNIT CAN MOVE IN THIS DIRECTION

PLASTIC HOUSING

"REFLECTOR"

ELECTRONIC UNIT

AUGMENTED EXD FLOW

ROTATION

FLYWHEEL

MAIN UNIT HOUSING

NORMAL g   ZERO g   3 g   ZERO g   NORMAL g

FIGURE II

(CROSS SECTIONAL VIEW AT "AA" - SEE FIG. I)

A

ELECTRONIC UNIT

POWER SUPPLY

BALL BEARING

FLYWHEEL

WORM & GEAR SPEED REDUCER

RUNSCHUR T MECH T

A

POWER OUTPUT SHAFT

FIGURE I.

would be very unhealthy if they should find out that you knew anything about it. If you knew the inside about some of the 'mine accidents', you'd realize how ruthless they are. Someone has found out something, and has decided to sing. Both gangs will stop fighting each other long enough to take care of a threat like that. Few people would believe the fellow if he did sing, but they don't take any chances. They could needle him insane, but it's easier and quicker to just have an accident. Mine accidents are so common that no one thinks there's anything peculiar about it. They kill a lot of other people besides the one they're after, of course, but a little thing like that doesn't bother them."

5-16 ('Uncle Bob"): "I wish you wouldn't try to do such damned impossible things with the machines you design! When we pick up your thoughts with problems like that on them, it's like setting a brand new puzzle in front of a cross word addict! That one last Tuesday had everyone down here beating their brains against their skull all week. Alan finally hit on the key, and the rest of us polished it up for you. It was interesting, but our own work took a beating. Alan is still young, but he's developing into a first rate technicon fast."

5-20 (Myia): "I don't like that book you're reading. Haven't you something there sort of light and romantic? Maybe you wouldn't like it, but I would. Hope you don't mind me bothering you, but I don't have anything to do just now except scan you. Iris knows it's lonesome enough here at best, and I have to do something for amusement once in a while, and Gibbon's Decline and Fall isn't exactly amusing!"

5-23 (Ira): 'We really don't know much more about the flying discs than you do. People down here have had them under almost constant observation, but I've never heard of one landing anywhere, or doing anything except to just look. Different ones have tried to communicate with them, but they won't answer. Myia tried to get a ray on them once, but they shorted it and then put out some sort of impervious force shield between us and their ship. Later, we detected their rays giving us the once over, but nothing happened, either then or later. They don't seem to be hostile, not at present, at least. Just nosey. They seem to be looking over all the cavern groups. Possibly looking for something or someone. Heard that some rod over in Washington state took a pot shot at one of them. Apparently damaged it some, but the others helped it away. They didn't even make any hostile moves against him. Just put out their force shied. Some say that they're just small craft, tenders or something, from a big ship. They claim that they've detected a mother ship high up."

5-29 (Myia): 'Have been visitng down under Tennessee. Getting up to date on my gossip. There are rumors that one of the gods was in the caverns recently. A young one. Sort of a routine inspection trip, or something of the sort. The older ones never seem to come here. The younger ones apparently have to spend a certain amount of time in such places as part of their apprentice training. Like a rookie officer having to spend a certain amount of time in some isolated post. He was interested in the cavern mech, as antiques! Some of it was so obsolete that he had trouble recognizing it. The Elders have improved mech which would clean up the caverns in a hurry, but it would be a major undertaking to transport it, and the necessary operators, here. He couldn't see much point in doing that just now. The same influences which created the present evil groups are still present, and would immediately begin to create new groups of the same sort. He promised to transmit the request to the Elder gods, but doubted that they would do anything at the present time. 'Later, perhaps'."

5-30 (Myia): 'There's a move on to try to organize all the 'white rays', but they're having more trouble than your United Nations. Uncle Bob was our delegate, but doesn't think anything will come of it. All are in favor of it, so long as they don't have to give up their own right to individual action. They're all too suspicious of each other. If there's to be a boss, each wants to be it. Instead of 'Let's cooperate together', it's 'You cooperate with us!'"

6-3 (Ira): "I think that you people will be permitted to develop inter-planetary travel, if you're able to do it. Others in this solar system do it, and the Elders don't seem to have any objections. I'm quite certain that you won't be allowed to develop real space travel outside of this planetary system. We're in quarantine. They don't want us wandering around in space, spreading our poisons. Those who come here from other systems apparently aren't allowed to return, with the exception of those who come here on official business for the gods."

6-12 (Myia): "Had a little trouble with some undesirable neighbors who wandered thru, but it's all O.K. now. They don't live here any more. Don't worry if you don't hear from us for a day or two at a time now and then. It doesn't necessarily mean that anything's wrong. There are a lot of reasons why we can't communicate exactly when we want to. Also, I have other work to do sometimes."

6-13 (Myia): "I like that tile bath you're doing. Wish I had one. Why don't you make it black and white? That's a pretty combination. My bath is an old wooden barrel, sawed in half. Sometimes I manage to get a small piece of soap. That's for special occasions only. Over under Bermuda, where we were visiting once, there's an ancient Elder bath still working. You should see it! Rays of some sort disintegrate all the dirt and dead skin off you. You come out feeling all aglow!"

"They used to use these same rays to do their laundry too. They will destroy any dead organic matter, but won't harm living or mineral matter. The Elders made their clothing out of mineral synthetics. It will clean rayon of nylong, but will destroy silk, cotton, or wool. They're all dead organics. They also used them to dispose of their garbage and sewage. The old mech used to reduce and purify all these wastes into their chemical elements, which could be used to synthize other things, but that part wasn't working when we were there."

6-15 (Myia): "Don't think the gardens and farms on the surface are going to do so good this year. Blame it on your bright scientists who just had to set off another atomic bomb! They're like kids playing with matches. It has a detrimental effect on the weather all over the world."

"We get our begetables from a big hydroponic garden under Cleveland. I think that there was some sort of ancient installation there, but it has been modernized in fairly recent times. The tanks are of ancient plastic, but the pipes are new -- monel metal, Ira says. They also have some modern pumps brought down from the surface. I forget the make. I'll put Ira on. Maybe he knows."

(Ira): "The pumps are Viking Model BM. I have the serial numbers, but they might trace them and cause someone some trouble. There are several hundred tons of modern hydroponic chemicals too. It cost someone plenty of money, if they paid for it. Don't know who put it in. There was no evidence of it having been used for several years, so we took over. They're very deep. There's no shortage of vegetables here, as long as we're able to get to them. We even raise enough to have a few chickens, but not enough for cattle, so the meat problem is still with us."

6-17 (Myia): "We're moving soon, temporarily, at least, so I'll

20

E X D (Gravity) M O T O R

By
Ira Amenophis, Tk.
and
R. M. Holland, M.E.

The following information was obtained by disassembling, as far
as practical, the driving unit of an antique wheeled vehicle. These
were used by the Ancients in their cities much as we use taxi-cabs.

The motivating force is the exd flow -- the constant stream of
finely divided matter, in the form of energy, which is constantly
attracted to our planet from space by the mass of the earth. The
friction of this flow, passing thru solid objects, is known to ortho-
dox science as "gravity". The denser the object, the greater the
resistance to the flow of exd and, consequently, the greater the
"weight" of the object.

Mechanically, the motor consists of a heavy flywheel mounted on
a shaft. In the original, this was made of some very dense material.
We had no equipment to test the actual hardness, but it could not be
marked with a small carborundum sharpening stone, altho it could be
scratched with a diamond.

The higher the speed of the flywheel, the greater the power it
will develop. It is, therefore, permitted to run at the highest
speed possible without danger of having it explode by centrifugal
force. Since this speed is toohigh to be used directly, the mech
included a two-stage speed reducer.

The first reduction consisted of a worm and wheel of unusual
design. (See Figure I) One firm has recently begun to manufacture
a worm unit somewhat similar to this, but not exactly the same. A
conventional worm and wheel unit could be substituted with a slight
loss of efficiency. Both the worm and wheel were made of the same
hard and dense material as the flywheel, and the working surfaces
were polished to a mirror finish.

The original unit had a further reduction, which is not shown
on the illustrations. This appeared to be similar to the hydraulic
drives, or "torque converters", used on some modern automobiles.
This was not disassembled because our time was limited, and because
it is not an essential part of the unit. Any desired output speed
could be obtained by several familiar methods.

The illustration shows the unit mounted on ball bearings, as the
bearings actually used on the original could probably not be dupli-
cated at the present time. They consisted of a number of flanged
cylinders which fit inside each other with only sufficient clearance
for an oil film. Each cylinder rotates at a slightly slower speed
than the one inside of it. Thus, while the speed of the shaft was
very high, the relative rubbing velocity between any two adjacent
surfaces was low. This would not theoretically reduce the total
friction, but it would keep the speeds low enough to permit maintain-
ing an oil film upon which the parts were "floated".

The exact nature of the lubricant is not known, but it makes the
mech almost frictionless. In one case where the original lubricant
was lost, it was replaced with "Prestone" silicone synthetic oil, to
which was added about 10% of another synthetic known as "Wynn's
Friction Proofing Oil." This was not quite as efficient as the original lubricant, and resulted in a higher temperature rise in the unit,
but can be used in case of necessity.

The "exd repelling" unit (See Figure II) is located over the flywheel in such a manner that one side of the wheel has no weight, and
the other side has triple weight. This causes it to rotate in the
direction shown by the arrow. The entire unit can slide, to cut down
the amount of power, or to make it rotate in the reverse direction.

It is on this unit that research must be done. It was entirely
encased in plastic, and could not be disassembled without destroying
it. Thus, all we could learn about it was what we were able to see
thru the plastic.

There were no tubes in the unit. There were, however, several
coils which were tapped off at different points. It is possible that
they function in the same manner as tubes, and could be replaced by
electronic tubes if desired. This technique of replacing tubes with
coils has just recently been "discovered" by the radio industry.

All the connections were very short, which would indicate that
it is a very high frequency set-up. The ray was radiated from a
trough shaped reflector, which was highly polished. This would also
indicate that the ray is in the semi-optical range. The plastic, so
far as our crude tests could indicate, apparently has about the same
characteristics as Polystyrene. We assumed that it was gas filled.

An unidentified "voice" once said that the principle was used by
every radio tube ever made, but would not explain further. One
technican partially verified this by saying that he thought that the
ray was similar to the electron flow from the filament to the plate
in a radio tube, but this was merely a deduction. Another called it
a "shading force", saying that it forced the normal flows out of
position in much the same manner that the shading poles on a motor
force the normal field out of position.

The power supply unit was also completely encased in plastic, so
that it also could not be disassembled without possibly destroying
it. This is not important, however, as conventional sources of power
could be used. Some of these machines generate power by dising air
or water. This particular power unit was apparently a power storage
device of some sort, as it had to be occasionally recharged from other
power sources. The power is transferred to the ray unit by means of
metal strips embedded in the plastic, one sliding on the other when
the unit moves.

The only limit on the speed of the flywheel is the load. If this
should be disconnected, the wheel would speed up until it burst. To
prevent this, the mech had a governor which would move the unit toward
the neutral center point when the speed exceeded a predetermined limit.
This is not shown on the illustration because the design would have
to change with each type of installation. The safe speed for a flywheel of any size or material can be computed from formulas found in
any engineering handbook. The design of a suitable governor mech
would be fairly simple.

The main problem is, of course, to discover the nature of the ray.
Once this is known, the rest would be easy. Such a ray would also
have many other uses, some of which might be even more important than
the exd motor. --- R.M.H. 11 March, 1949.

have to stop my little visits with you. An uncle and his group over under Indiana need some help. Some undesirable neighbors have moved in near them. They could handle it themselves, but some of the group are away just now. With us to help them, it shoudl be easy. We'll stay with them until they're all together again, and then move on. We might come back here, or we might go somewhere else. It all depends. Better keep your notes on our conversations to yourself for a while. They might do both you and us a lot of harm if they fell into the wrong hands."

7-13 (Myia): 'We're back again, for a little while. The clean up job was tougher then we expected, so we brought our relatives here. When the rest of the family gets here, we'll have another try. It's O.K. to copy your notes to send to Shaver. From what I've heard, he can be trusted with them. There probably won't be anything new in them, as he's had a lot of cavern contact. The only thing is that I want to look them over as you copy them. There are some things that I might want to cut out. Also, don't actually send them until I give the word."

7-14 (Myia): 'I don't think Eisenhower will be a candidate for either party-He doesn't want the job, and some friends down here are working on him to strengthen his decision. They want him to be available for some much more important work if he should be needed when the Russian trouble breaks out. A President gets too involved in too many different problems to concentrate on one, and there's too much tamper in Washington to depend too much on anyone there. They're picking out a lot of people the same way. Influential people, or specialists in their line, just in case. I don't think there's been any open contact with any of them. They don't know what they've been picked out. They've merely been selected and their thinking gently guided into the desired channels. It's not really a make ray that they're using. A real friend wouldn't, unless it was almost a matter of life or death. Too much make ray and your own brain becomes almost useless. You become a ro-man. Run those together and put a capital letter on it. Now figure it out. It will be good exercise for you."

'The Russian affair may come to a head any time now. I don't know whether it will include a surface war too. There's always been a lot of very evil surface contact in Russia. They used to have an agreement with the Imperial government and the church. The cavern rods kept them informed about things, and did other odd jobs for them. In return, the government and church kept them well supplied with slaves, particularly women. The Russian caverns were the bigest white slave syndicate in the world. They kept the most desirable ones for themselves, and sold the others all over the world, after they had ray-trained them. Some of them appeared on the surface again, as prostitutes or 'bird dogs', to earm money for their owners, or to lure other people into their reach."

'There was a 'palace revolution' in the Russian caverns and, for several years, they were too busy fighting each other to bother about the surface. During the time, the surface people took advantage of the situation to overthrow both the government and the church, and the Bolsheviks came into power."

'The new cavern bosses finally made a deal with Stalin and his gang. Joe thought he could use them as long as it suited his plans, and then dump them. They've given him a lot of help, and have been well paid for it. Joe has a lot of enemies that he's willing to toss to them. The famous purge was their work. The way the suspects got up and talked themselves right into an execution cell was a dead give away. Make ray. Then they began to process the Communist leaders and key party men in other countries. Joe would invite them to Russia, as a 'special honor', and the rods would ray train them into ros for the party -- and for the cavern bosses, only Joe didn't know that latter part! For many years now, they've been slipping gangs thru the caverns to strategic points all over the world. It's easy to do. Several thousand could slip in here, and no one would know it unless they accidentally saw them, or unless they began to work here. Some groups are active, but there are many others who are supposed to be laying low until they're needed. How many, no one knows. People who talk about the 'Communist underground' are speaking truer than they know!"

'The new bosses over there have ambitions. They want to rule the whole world. Stalin is now finding out what so many others have found out before him -- when you tie up with a gang of cavern rods, it isn't them that get used! They're now running both Russia and the Communist parties. Everything the Russians do is designed to forward the bosses' plans for conquest. They're gradually spreading out, both on the surface and underground, and getting set for the big push. The U.S. is the prime objective. It's the biggest plum. After that, the others will come easy. You people have a lot of friends here who will do what they can to help. Even some of the rod and goon squads will resist. They don't want to see the Russian bosses win. It would interfere with their own plans. When thieves fall out --. Others will help the invaders."

'Your people wouldn't believe that they're in such great danger if they were told. Your whole civilzation is in danger, but you people are so smug and complacent that it's sickening! You engineers especially! You're so damned proud of all your semi-rbot mech which is the bais of your civilization. You never stop to think how vulnerable you've made yourselves by making it. Your whole lives actually depend on the continued operation of this mech. Without it, there would be chaos before you could regear your lives to do without it. It wouldn't be so bad if it were really robot mech, but it's only semi-robot. The real brain of it is still human. A few men have to be on the job to make adjustments from time to time to keep it running, and to direct it. Their jobs are so technical that no one else could do them without a long period of training. Your lives are really in the hands of these few technicons. They're reliable, and all that, but they're human."

"Just as an example, the water supply of New York City depends on about a dozen very highly trained men. No one could take their jobs over in an emergency. If they should all stop work at the same time, the water supply would get into such a mess that it would stop within a day or two. When the water supply stops, the sewage disposal system also stops. When that happens, the city becomes uninhabitable within 48 hours or so, because of disease epidemics. Result: A panic stricken mass exodus. Mobs roaming the countryside looking for food, wasting more than they use. Highways clogged. Possibly a few old 'junkers' driven by enemy agents, and disabled at the right spots to tie things up."

'That's just one example. The same thing could happen in any one of a hundred other cities. Transport, communications, and public utilities could all be tied up the same way. You people don't realize the danger, but your enemies do! A few quick blasts by some rods hidden for that very purpose, and the job is done. Don't think for a moment that they would hesitate to do it. You can't realize how absolutely evil and ruthless these things down here are. Their gangs on the surface would be just as bad. They've been ray trained until they're not really human any more. They're merely tools of the Russian bosses. They'll do as they're ordered, no matter how evil or horrible, without a second thought. The ones you have to fear aren't the loud mouthed crackpots. The real ones haven't shown their hands yet. They may be working and living beside you, without being recognized."

'Such a situation would be exactly what the Russian bosses want. It would give them your cities and industrial mech undamaged by warfare. They wouldn't have to invade. Your new rulers are probably already here. Some of them may be respected public figures. All this may never happen. I hope not. It may be stopped before you ever learn anything about it. But the danger is real. It's terrible. I wish there was some way I could make people realize just how terrible it is."

'When the blow up comes, if it does, the safest places will be the most worthless places. The mountains or forests. Places that have nothing of military or economic value to attract the enemy. Some of the technicons at Oak Ridge have been convined of the danger, but I don't think they really know where the information came from. They've built refuge centers disguised as hunting and fishing lodges. Food, supplies, defense munitions and technical mech for several years stay has been hidden there. Routes to these places have been worked out to avoid cities and other places weres traffic might get tied up. Fuel and other emergency supplies are cached at idsguised summer cottages along the way. It may all seem far fetched, but if you really knew these stinkers, you'd agree with me."

7-15 (Myia): 'You're not making much progress copying your notes, and I've a lot more to give you while I have the chance. Get busy. I'll see that no one bothers you, except me!"

'You have the wrong idea about the Elder's religion. You can't really call it a religion, because it was no mystery to them. They understood these things, and why they were so, so they were merely part of their scientific facts to them. The lesser ones, and those who came later, didn't have the mental capacity to unde stand. It was all a big mystery to them, and they got a distorted idea of things. So it became a religion."

7-20 (Myia): 'Shaver's story, 'Titan's Daughter', was very interesting. I always enjoy stories about robots. None of our group have ever seen one in working order, but the ancients really used to have them. I can remember hearing about robots as far back as I can remember anything, but a lot of the stories are pure fiction. Down here they make up robot stories to amuse the children, just as your people make up fairy stories for yours. The only part of the story that I'd question is about the 'mind city' acting as it did. The ancient robots couldn't harm a human. In fact, they couldn't even let any harm befall a human if they could prebent it, even at the cost of their own existence. That was the master control, which would block out all other controls if necessary."

'You have the wrong idea about the word 'sol', the ancient word for the sun. It has no evil meaning. It's strictly good. 'Sunlife-source'. It means that the sun is the source of all life, the means by which the Sacred Four, at the command of the Nameless One, created life upon this earth. 'The rays of the sun met the rays of the earth in the mud of the seas, and generated life germs from the particles of mud. From these, came forth life in the waters, as had been commanded. Then the rays of the sun met the rays of the earth in the dust of the land, and generated lnfe germs from the particles of dust. From these, cam forth life upon the land, as had been commanded.' The ancients made their words count! One word covered the whole story of creation."

'Sun is also good. 'Sun-you-seed'. The sun caused you to be born and to grow. The sun te and the earth te must meet to generate life and growth. That's why I don't go entirely for the theory that the gods went to a dark planet, in spite of the fact that some tapes say so. Life which already existed could continue, but they would have to create a synthetic sun te before there could be new life and growth. Synthetic things are seldom as perfect as the natural. They usually omit one or two little things which later turn out to be important. There are suns outside the present 'tide of de'. It would seem much more sensible to go to a planet with a ben sun."

'The word 'desolate', which he cites, is comething else again. 'de', bad - 'sol', which I've already explained - 'ate', animal te. Both 'sol' and 'animal te' have been 'dee-d'. They have been engulfed by the 'tide of de'. The whole story of the greatest tragedy in human histroy symbolized by one word! 'Sun-day' - 'the sun is now de to animals, why?' After the great catastrophe, people didn't have much time for reflection on the past. But they didn't want to forget the past entirely. So one day a week was set aside to study the ancient lore, to reflect on the glories of the gods who were now gone, and the reasons for their present state. Gradually it got changed into the worship of the gods themselves, and became part of their 'religion'."

What he says about bodies encased in platic is true. I've seen many of them. They say that ships sometimes come here, search out one or two particular bodies, and take them away. Relatives or friends rescuing someone who was left behind, possibly."

'Shaver has often said that the moon fall caused the Biblical flood. It did, but there's a long story between the two events. The start and end result of a chain reaction, as it were. It happened during what your scientists call the tertiary era. There weren't supposed to be any humans on earth then, but there were. A higher grade of humans than we have now."

'There were two moons at that time, the present one, whose orbit was much further out than it is now, and a much larger one nearer the earth. I call them 'moons', but they were really planets. It was a triplex planetary system. This larger moon was inhabited, and the inhabitants called it 'Azatlan'. The earthmen sometimes called it the 'Star of Bal', but that wasn't really a name at all. It merely meant that animal-life existed there."

'At that time, there were no mountains on the earth, just the seas and gently rolling land. Under the land at various points, and at varying depths, were huge chambers, or caverns, filled with explosive gasses which had been formed when the earth was formed. The gods knew that these pockets existed, and that they were dangerous, which is one of the many reasons why they build their cities so far underground -- far below these gas pockets."

'When the gods came to the earth, the most suitable and fruitful land area for the surface portion of their settlement was in the Pacific. So far as I can find out, this was originally called Mu, but others seem to refer to it as 'Pan', 'Lemuria', and so on. 'Mu', which the ancients pronounced 'moo', meant 'mother'. It was the original motherland on Earth, because the gods first settled there -- the Garden of Eden of your Bible. The high regard for the cow as a symbol of motherhood by early people seems to come from the fact that it says 'moo'. From Mu, they spread out both east and west, both on the surface and underground. Mu was the motherland. The others were colonies."

'The orbit of Azatlan grew constantly smaller, and it began to lose its air and water to the stronger gravitation of Earth. Many of the people migrated to Earth, and founded an island settlement in theAtlantic -- Atlantis. They also spread out, both on the surface and underground. They established colonies in the Mediterranean area -- only it was dry land then -- as far east as Egypt, where they met the only colonists who had come west from U. Eventually, the tunnel systems of the two also met, and they seem to have mingled on very friendly terms. "

"I'm not certain that any of the present human races originated on Earth. There are some records which say that the Negro races evolved, with elder god aid, from earth life forms, and that all other races either migrated here, or are cross breeds between the two. The eldergods from Mu were a light blond race, altho the records say they brought some other peoples with them, but in small numbers. The Atlans were dark. The yellow-red races are also supposed to have come from a moon, but not Azatlan. Maybe from our present moon, when it was further out, and had air and water on it. The Nors were also here at one time, but they seem to have been more visitors than settlers. They were very light. 'Norman' -- 'Norsemen' -- 'Nordic' -- these words all came from the Nors. They were so highly regarded that people were proud to claim Nor blood -- even with a Bar-sinister! "

'To get on with the main story again, Azatlan kept coming closer to Earth until it finally reached what your scientists call 'Roche's limit'. At this point, the conflicting gravitational forces rent it to pieces. The fragments began to circle the earth in a ring, which also kept coming closer to Earth, until the larger fragments began falling on us. Some of them also went outward, and eventually fell on the present moon. In fact, the moon took a worse beating than Earth. That's why it is so scarred up. Some of the fragments are still circling the earth. Your scientists are just discovering it. The elder gods knew it ages ago. "

'Some of these flaming meteors crashed into the gas pockets, and caused them to blow up. Among these were the shallow pockets under a surface Mu. After violent earthquakes and volcanic acticity, the thin surface crust collapsed, and the whole continent fell into the sea of fire at the bottom of the cavern. The ocean rushed in, and boiled and seethed over the spot for many months. Later, the same thing happened to Atlantis. The meteors and volcanic activity continued for a long time. The records aren't specific. Just 'a long time'. Where the pockets were near the surface, the land sank into the sea. Where they were deeper, the crust was thick enough to stay in its heaved up position, forming the mountains. The gasses from the deeper pockets seeped into the cavities left by this upheaving, and formed our present 'volcanic belts'. Our present volcanos form the safety vents of these belts. "

'The coming of the 'tides of de' had something to do with it, but the records are rather sketchy on this point. At any rate, the gods knew what was going to happen, and it seems that this was one of the reasons why they were leaving the earth. It seems that perhaps they misjudged the time of the blow up slightly. Or maybe those who really knew had already gone, and the ones who were left didn't have brains enough to figure it right. Their cities and tunnels were deep enough to be safe, but it seems that they didn"t get the barriers up in time. The poison gas swept thru the caverns, and killed most of the people in them. There were some survivors both on the surface and in the caverns, but they were only a small fraction. Atlantis didn't seem to suffer as much as Mu. Maybe the reaction wasn't as violent there. Or maybe, with the example of Mu before them, they were better prepared. More of them survived, and Atlantis replaced Mu as the cultural center of the earth for a while. Finally it too went down, and the age of the gods ended. "

"The Biblical flood was the least of the troubles. With all the upset, it's no wonder that there were gigantic tidal waves, and upset weather conditions, to add to the misery of the survivors.

After the catastrophe, those who were left were forced down into
savagry. It was then that canibalism began. 'Man ate the fruit
of the tree of life', your Bible says. Man was the fruit of the
tree of life. He was so represented in the ancient god symbolism.
So it meant that man ate man. They had nothing else to eat. All
their usual sources of food had been destroyed."

'Our present moon will eventually break up and fall on the earth.
The planets will all eventually break up and fall onto the sun
the same way. It's the law of the Nameless One. All things go
in cycles. All things must return to their source to begin again.
After the planets have all returned to the sun, the sun will expand
into a dust cloud -- a super nova, your scientists would call it.
Then the etheric currents will gather the dust into swirling clouds,
which will condense into a new planetary system, and we start all
over again. But you don't have to worry. The process takes many
millions of million years.''

'The moon? Yes, there's still life there, but no human life. What
water and atmosphere are left there are on the dark side of the
moon, held there by centrifugal force, as water is held in a bucket
when you whirl it on the end of a rope. The life forms there are
crude now, fungi and so on. I didn't get this from elder records.
Space travellers have told me all I know about it. Don't think
there's much, if anything on the surface of the moon now. It's
all underground. Natural caverns, connected by short tunnels.
Space travellers use it as sort of an emergency base. There might
be signs of the former inhabitants there, but space travellers
aren't much interested in such things."

7-21 (Myia) (Commenting on story 'New Face, Same Heel', in
Amazing Stories): 'The basis of the story is not impossible. The
physical body and the kui are entirely separate entitles. The kui
is not material in the sense that you can weigh it or measure it,
but it is a definate force. It's material in the same sense that
electricity is material. When the physical body dies, the kui
seeks a new host body, usually a baby about to be born. The transfer does not have to be made immediately. The physical body can
exist, in a mechanical sort of way, without a kui for a time, and
a kui can exist for a time without a host body. When a kui enters
an infant's body, it loses its conscious memory. Its previous experiences are buried in its subconscious.''

'A kui can also enter an adult body whose kui is temporarily ab-
sent. They do leave the host body at times, and can be temporarily
driven out by great fright. When a kui enters an adult's body this
way, it retains its previous memories. They say that the latter-
gods were able to put their kuis into another body. When their
own bodies became aged or diseased, they would transfer to the body
of some young, healthy person. The old superstitions about a person
being possessed by 'de-viles' had its basis in fact. It would be
only a 'de-vile' or 'de-man' who would do such a thing. A friend
wouldn't treat anyone like that. Possibly this story is a tip-off
to the fact that someone has rediscovered this old art. I really
wouldn't know.''

'The kui is independent of the limitations of time and space. If
it can't find a suitable host body on this planet, it may seek one
on another. I don't know how long it can remain disembodied. Some
tapes say it can remain in this state almost indefinately, and that
what you call 'spirits' really do exist. I've been rather doubtful
about this. I've seen so much fraud and trickery by your 'mediums',
often with cavern aid, that it may have blinded me to the truth.''

'You don't believe in reincarnation. I know that it is so, because
I've often sutdied the details of someone's previous incarnation.
They don't consciously remember it, but it's there. You can bring

26

it out with ray mech. I've done it many times. It could also be done with hypnotism, but not as easily. If you know a good hypnotist, who is willing to take the time to really try it, you can prove it yourself."

'You can get thru to some people easier than others. If their past lives have been happy and good, the details come out quite easily. It may be necessary to make several tries, in order to condition them for it, before you get good results. Sometimes you will run up against a violent block. You can redognize it because there will be an atmosphere of intense horror. You can't force such a block, and if you try you are likely to needle the subject insane. Also caution your hypnotist to have the subject forget all he's said when he awakens. Otherwise it may result in multiple-identity and insanity."

'Kui is pronounced 'koo-ee' -- your inherent and potential personal energy -- the stuff that makes you tick. It's a force of some sort, part of the universal and infinate force which the Elders called the 'Nameless One'. If we had the mental capacity of the gods, and had studied it for thousands of years, as they did, we would be able to understand the exact nature of the kui. As it is, the 'Nameless One' must continue to remain nameless to us."

'The natives of the South Sea Islands and Australia use 'cooee' as a hailing call. Their ancestors were survivors from Mu, and the word comes directly from the old Elder work 'kui'. They're hailing the real inner self of the person when they call that, but they probably don't know it. You'll find evidences of the old Elder culture all over the world, particularly in the woods, customs and legends of the primitive peoples. They've preserved the old lore, but most of them have long since forgotten the meanings."

7-22 (Myia): 'I've been giving yoo some long conversations to copy, but there's so much that I want to tell you, and I may not have much time to do it. The things over under Indiana are spreading out. They're under western Ohio now. We're vulnerable here and may have to move suddenly unless the rest of our relatives arrive sooner than we expect. There are nine groups of us scattered around the U.S., all related. Most of them are technicons of some sort. When grandfather was alive, he kept them fairly well together, but now that he's gone they've sort of split up and drifted around. We all work together when needed, but sometimes it takes time to get them together."

'I don't really know what happens to the kui of those people whose bodies are encased in plastic. They say that when they are revived, their own original kui returns to their body. Maybe it sort of goes into suspended animation too."

'What you call personality and individuality is mostly physical. Each kui has a certain amount of individuality, but not so marked or intense as that due to physical differences. It's all a matter of chemical balances. The Elders understood these well, and compounded their foods accordingly. They would put in extra amounts of chemical elements which would bring out certain characteristics, according to the activity they intended to engage in. Some of your doctors have recently rediscovered this art. You can find it in modern books and magazines on diet, so I won't take time to repeat it."

7-23 (Myia): 'The kui can, and often does, leave its host body. It might go anywhere. As I told you, it's independent of the limitations of time and space. It can travel across the universe as easily and as quickly as across the room. When the physical body sleeps, the kui may go wandering around on its own. When you dream of being someplace, maybe your kui really was there. Or maybe someone down here was just playing around with some mech, for their own amusement, or yours. It's almost impossible to tell which.''

'The hypnotist you're thinking about probably actually did send his subject's kui to the caverns. (Note: Letter in Amazing Stories) It's a dangerous thing to do. It's always dangerous to send any-one's kui on a trip. When it goes of its own accord, as when you're asleep, it's conditioned to return to its own body. When it's snet, it's under no such compulsion, unless the hypnotist has previously so conditioned it. It might find someplace it liked better than its old body, and not return. Then the physical body would die, and the hypnotist would have some very embarrasing questions to answer. There's more danger of this right now than before. Most people are under great pressure, and secretly long to 'get away from it all'. They might take advantage of the possibilityand do exactly that.''

'Even under the best conditions, with the subject carefully condi-tioned and all, there's always danger. Something might frighten the kui so badly that it would get confused and not try to get back. It might not be conditioned for what it saw. I wouldn't recommend that anyone try it, but if they do, they should start in a small way. Send the subject's kui to another room, or to some other place they know is safe, and then gradually extend their tours. You don't take a car out on a crowded highway the first time you try to drive it, do you?''

''As I said, it's dangerous to send anyone's kui to the caverns, and would probably also be useless. The chances are that they'd see no one. Most of the caverns are uninhabited. There are only a few places where groups have anything like a permanet settlement. It's mostly nomadic groups just wandering around and stopping for a while where they find conditions to their liking. On the other hand, they might see anything. And I do mean literally anything. There are life forms down here that are so fantastic that you wouldn't believe them unless you saw them. If they did meet any-one, it might be just too bad. A few groups might be friendly, but a lot of them aren't. ''

'The Oriental mystics and American Indians who send their kuis on journeys do so by a sort of self-hypnotism. The fasting, mystic rites, and all the other membo-jumbo they go thru has nothing to do with it actually. That may be their way of obtaining the necessary degree of concentration, or it may merely be part of their act.''

7-25 (Ira): 'The ancient god language was almost entirely symbolic. The ordinary people couldn't read it because they didn't know the meaning of the symbols. The gods would teach these things to those whom they deemed worthy, but they weren't available to everyone. You had to be selected. Later, after the gods had left, students tried to translate the symbolic records into plain language. Whether they did it correctly or not is the subject of a lot of argument. There's a lot of disagreement between the different tapes on the subject.''

'Man was always symbolized as a peculiar sort of goat. Actually, the symbol looks more like some sort of deer or antelope, but all the tapes call it a goat. We've never been able to find out the signi-ficience of the symbol, but there were actually goat-men in the old days. I've seen their preserved bodies. This symbolic goat is al-ways pictured as leaping upon the land. Other forms of life are pictured as evolving, but man is always pictured as leaping upon the land fully developed. The only logical deduction is that they came here from some place else.''

'My, the original motherland, is symbolized as a tree -- the tree
of life. The Unnamable is pictured as an adorned serpent, usually
feathered, bearded, crowned, or adorned in some manner. An un-
adorned serpent merely symbolizes water -- the sea. Students believe that each different form of adornment has a different meaning,
but don't know what. When pictured in the role of Creator, the
serpent has seven heads, probably because the world was created in
seven different stages, according to the old records. No doubt the
Biblical seven days also comes from this. "

'The top four gods, the Sacred Four, were symbolized as four
pillars. You'll find this four pillar symbol incorporated in many
of the ancient temples. They remembered the symbol, even if they
did forget the meaning. There's a story behind each of the symbols, but only the gods know the story in some cases. "

7-26 (Myia): 'The power of the kui is unlimited, if only you
could learn to direct it. You would probably call it 'mind over
matter'. The kui usually acts thru the various organs of the
physical body, but it doesn't necessarily have to. There have
been cases where people whose eyes have been destroyed can see
with their fingers, or some other part of their body. Cases where
people live and think normally with their brain gone. Your doctors
don't talk about the, because they can't explain them., but they're
recorded in their medical histories. Rays under the war zones have
seen men who bodies were completely shattered heal themselves and
go on to complete their mission. The old advice about 'pulling
yourself together' is based on possibility. "

'The whole secret is concentration -- not as you use the word, but
total and complete concentration on one subject, to the absolute
exclusion of all other subjects. The wounded soldiers were so
swayed by the hysteria of the battle that they attained the necessary degree of concentration automatically. Thus their kuis
were able to do things which would normally be impossible for them.
The gods used to spend thousands of years trying to train themselves so that they could attain this degress of perfection at
will. They never completely succeeded, with the possible exception
of the top group -- the Sacred Four. We can't hope to even begin.
Our lives aren't long enough. "

7-28 (Myia): 'We're moving at once. We might be back some time,
but I can't say when. If any of us ever get within range of you
again, we'll let you know, but it may be some time. "

'Yes, it's O.K. to send your notes to Shaver if you want to, but I
don't see much point in it. If he's in touch with groups here,
there won't be much in them that's new to him. But you can do it
if it will make you feel any better. Only wait a couple of months.
Some one whom we wouldn't care to meet might see it and recognize
us. If they did, they might scan your brain and get some leads as
to where to find us. You've a lot more information in your head
than you've set down in your notes, altho you don't realize it.
But they could find it. In a couple of months, the trail will be
too cold to follow, and we'll be in a safe place even if they did
follow it. So wait a couple of months before you tell anyone
about it. "

* * * * *

All the planets did a few flip-flops getting their orbits readjusted, and several of them ended up by spinning on a new axis. Terra's north pole, for instance, used to be somewhere in southern in southern U.S."

"The people on the other planets are determined that it isn't going to happen again, if they can prevent it. They want to stop any further development, and safely dispose of the bombs that have already been made. A few "accidents' to your atomic piles and some of the scientists would take care of the first part ordinarily, but there are complications. You see, Joe has 'em too! If they begin liquidating in either Russia or the U.S., they're likely to think the other is attacking them, and soon they'll be tossing A-bombs at each other."

"Disposing of the present stocks of bombs is the tough part. They don't want to simply blow them up, as that would stir up the sun still more, and they don't know how to deactivate them. I heard that they have appealed to the Elders for technical information and advice. In the meantime, they're just watching and trying to keep everyone concerned calmed down. Notice how the Oak Ridge technicons have clammed up recently? Maybe a few of them have been confidentially told something. Some of the groups here have. Some of the mad rods would like to get something started just for the hell of it, but they've sort of slapped a few of them down. Wish they'd help us clean all of them out!"

"All of your funny weather isn't due to the A-bombs. According to the old tapes, this is the start of the ebb of the flow of de, and there is likely to be a certain natural increase in sun spot activity for a few years. The bomb is stirring it up even more than this natural increase, however. There will be some reaction later. Every action causes a reaction. The flow of de is now abnormal, so will eventually become sub-normal for a while. So there's some compensation if the thing can be stopped before it causes a real disaster."

1-7-49 (Myia): "The interior of the earth is naturally cold. Some of the deeper parts are solid ice now. The main source of surface heat is the sun. That penetrates below the surface for a certain distance, and averages up to a mean temperature, but, below that point, it gets very cold. The only internal sources of heat are radioactive pockets, which we stay away from and the volcanic belts. These volcanic belts are usually under the mountainous regions, and most of your deep mines are in the mountains. That's why they get hotter as they go deeper. They're getting nearer the volcanic belt. Some cavern settlements are located near these volcanic belts, in order to take advantage of the heat. It's O.K. so long as you don't get close enough to be in danger of the gasses which might seep in."

The Elders also had various ways of heating the colder parts of the caverns. The most popular means was a sort of reverse refrigeration process. Your technicons are familiar with the process, only they've never done it on such a huge scale. This mech is still working in some places, and we usually try to get to heated parts of the caverns, if we can. The 'blowing caves' on the surface are probably vents from this mech in many cases, particularly if the air is cold. You couldn't get in or out that way. At least, not without a major construction job. They were purposely built so that nothing but air could pass thru. In some places, they let the air seep out thru porous rock formations."

1-14-49 (Ira) "I managed to get thru on a relay, very briefly, to a technicon who gave me some more information on the subject of controlling natural forces and energy flows. This is the basis of most of the mech down here. What he told me tells what to do, but you'll have to figure out how to do it, as we don't know. It's going to be a little difficult for me to explain it, as we don't speak the same language. The only Elder units and terms which we use would mean nothing to you, and I don't know the surface technical cant too well. However, I(ll try, and hope someone can understand what I'm trying to say."

"On a piece of graph paper, lay out a hyperbolic curve, with its focus at one corner, and its asymptote extending upward. This represents fairly accurately how the natural energy flows increase in amplitude, or power. Now draw a straight vertical line so that it cuts the upper part of the curve; up where the curve is running almost straight up. This line represents the energy applied by the mech. The curve is a constant. The straight vertical line is variable in a horizontal direction. Because the angle between the two lines is so small, a very slight change in the position of the vertical cut-off line will produce a large change in the height of the cut-off point on the curve, thus representing a considerable change in the strength of the natural energy flow. This represents graphically the manner in which come of the mech 'triggers', or controls, natural flows."

"In the case of the gravity powered mech, some sort of force, or field, pulls the natural gravity flow out of its normal path. This applied force might be called a 'shading' force. It pulls the natural flow out of normal position in much the same manner that a 'shading' pole will pull the normal magnetic poles of a motor around. Only, in this case, the force isn't magnetic, of course."

"I asked about the remark you heard, regarding the secret being used in radio tubes. He wasn't sure, but thinks the flow used to divert gravity is very similar to the electron flow from the filment to the plate in a radio tube. There are no tubes in a gravity diverting mech, but there are quite a few coils of various sorts, and it is possible that some of these perform the same functions as tubes."

"We're on our way back to our gardens under-Cleveland for a few days. Will contact you when we get there."

1-15-49 (Myia): 'We're back for a couple of days to collect food and other supplies we had hidden here. Then we're taking off for another locality. Can't tell you how soon we'll be back. Maybe six months; maybe a year. Don't dare tell you where we're going, but it's too far to contact yo, from there. Sorry, but it's very important to sus to go there. Don't think you'll have any serious trouble while we're away. There's nothing really bad right near here just now, and Ira always disables the mech when we leave. The goons don't have brains enough to reactivate it, so any tamper would have to be long range, and couldn't be very powerful."

"Only a small part of the tamper comes from the made rods. Most of it is just someone down here playing around. Something like kids who pull wings off flies, or legs off grasshoppers, or tie tin cans to the tails of dogs. From the kids' point of view, it's just something to do; just something to pass the time away. From the flies' and grasshoppers' and dogs' point of view, it's serious deviltry. There are plenty down here who have the bodies of adults, but the minds of 7 or 8 year old spoiled brats. What makes it tough is that they also have the mech of the gods."

"I promised to tell you about Adam. In the first place, Adam wasn't an individual. It was the name of a group; the first of the present human race. The ancients, particularly the Hebrews, from whom the story of Adam and Eve came, had the habit of personifying cities or tribes as one individual. People still do it, to a certain extent. You refer to the English people collectively as 'John Bull', and so on. Adam -- 'a de animal-man'. Apparently, a very inferior grade of humanity."

"'Eve' is incorrect. The name was originally JeviJ -- e-vi -- which is self explanatory. The name forms the base of several other words. 'Levi' -- the life that came from Evi. Some of the higher gods were 'devine' -- de-vi-n -- their 'vi', or 'personal magnetism' was so great that they were de to the seed (or descendants) of Evi. In other words, they were de to the ordinary humans. They couldn't be closely approached."

"The story of Adam is nearly all in your Bible, if you know how to interpret what you read, and read between the lines now and then. There are several things which you have to keep in mind."

"First, remember what I told you about Ezra, and his translations. The symbols, or glyphs, which the Elders used, and which Moses used, are very complicated. There are many minor varieties of each one, each with a slightly different meaning. A person who really knows them, may spend several minutes putting a dozen or so of them into words. Erza didn't know the variations. He only caught the basic meansings, which makes his version sketchy and incomplete. If that didn't make sense, he just juggled it around until it did. In a few places, this changes the meaning badly. In other places, it puts events out of their right sequence and order."

"Second, the older parts of your Bible refer mainly to the Elder gods. At that time, the present humans were not important enough to rate more than an occasional mention. Jehovah was an Elder god; the tribal god of the Hebrews. The 'giants', 'sons of God', 'angels', and prophets, were all Elders."

"Third, don't take times and dates too literally. Exact months and years weren't important to a race that measured their ages in eons. Yards and miles were very unimportant details to people who could go all over space."

"The Adams were the product of the Elder biological laboratories; a cross between the Elder races and a man-like beast which was native to Terra. I'm using 'Elder races' loosely, to indicate the Elders, Atlans, Nors, and all the others."

"Eventually, the Adams began to pick up too many Elder secrets, and the Elders feared that they might also learn the secret of prolonging their lives indefinately. So they took them out of the caverns, and put them up on the surface. It wasn't that the Elders were really stingy with this secret. They intended to give it to them later. That was one of Yahveh's purposes. But they didn't want to 'fix the type' until they had improved. That's all in the Bible. Somewhat garbled, but it's there."

"There seems to have been a lot more Elder blood added after the Adams went up on top. The boys must have liked their women wild, because they were always tom-catting around on the surface. Your Bible says: 'the sons of God saw the daughters of men, that they were fair, and they took them wives of all they chose.' The ancient Hebrew version says: 'They lay with all they chose.' Somewhere along the line between the ancient Hebrew and the modern English version someone made honest women out of them."

32

1-16-49 (Cyril): "Before we go, I'll give you some additional comment on some of the subjects which I've discussed. It might be possible to administer the radioactive decontamination treatment orally, but my own thought is that it would have to be intravenously. If the process ever becomes common, it is going to raise a problem of how to safely dispose of the wastes. If they just put them in the sewage disposal system, it will eventually contaminate the water supply."

"The Elders used to extract the radioactive poisons from various substances by centrifuging them at very high speeds. All of this radioactive 'garbage' was loaded into robot controlled space ships, which were sent to certain specified spots in open space, where they blew up. These spots were well away from all planetary systems, and space ship routes, so that the stuff couldn't do any damage. Your astronomers have recently discovered some of these places, and term them 'hot spots'. They're 'hot' in more ways than one!"

"Your research workers and medicons would also have to take care that their 'absorbing' compounds were 'clean'. They'd tend to pick up natural radioactivity, and might have to be decontaminated before they could be used."

"Regarding the virus diseases, several of them, polio in particular, are what you could technically call 'filth diseases'. That is, they are eliminated in the feces, from where they are transmitted to other host bodies. A few varieties can be air-borne, but most of them are water and food borne. In the presence of high or low temperatures, they simply revert to lower forms, and become inactive, so it would be difficult to kill them in this manner. They do require a certain amount of time to revert, however, so it might be possible to kill them if the change of temperature could be applied very suddenly."

1-16-49 (Myia): "Here's a tip for your cave explorers, or anyone else who suspects ray activity. Nearly all the rays will register on photographic film or paper. So carry a piece of unexposed film or paper, wrapped in light proof paper, in your hat, or someplace around your head. On your return, develop it and look for ray marks. They might be in the form of lines or spots, or there might be a general fogging of the whole thing, depending on how near the ray was. They might put a ray on you without touching the paper, but if it's marked, you know a ray was there."

"Only don't use color film or paper, unless you can develop it yourself. If it goes back to the manufacturer for processing, and is ray marked, you'll never see it. You'll probably get a polite note back saying that it was defective in manufacture, and maybe a free replacement of the raw film. This is a confidential policy of the international film cartel, adopted at the insistence of the German members. They don't seem to care about black and white, but seem to be afraid of color for some reason. Maybe the color of a ray mark would give a clew to its frequency or nature. This is only a guess, I don't really know."

1-16-49 (Q): "It always seemed to me that the Fortean Society and the Shaver Mystery Club were natural tie-ins. Yet, Tiffany Thayer wrote me that they took no notice of the Shaver Mystery because it was merely fiction, presented frankly as such, and it was not the function of the Society to act as literary critics. In the last issue of 'Doubt', a member wrote in pointing out that Shaver claimed that it was true, and that a number of non-fiction articles had now been added. Thayer ignored this part of the letter, and gave his standard 'fiction' story again. Do you happen to know why?"

Myia: "We're taboo! The caverns are Damned! There seems to be a growing trend in the Fortean Society, which I hate to see, to make a religion out of it. If it isn't mentioned in 'The Books', it doesn't exist. Fort never mentioned the caverns in his books, so cavern data is excluded."

"I've always wondered why Fort didn't mention the caverns. They tell me that he knew. That's fairly obvious from his books. A person could scarcely skirt around a subject so closely without accidentally touching it, unless they knew all about it and were deliberately avoiding it. Much of his data is clearly ray work. Othere data is of extraterrestrial activities. Possibly he considered them a greater menace than the cavern activities, and wanted to focus attention on on them."

"Or maybe he just wasn't ready to die. Much of his work was done in London. At that time they tell me that the rods and hoods were running things with a high hand over there. Their motto was: 'To know, is to die.' They enforced it strictly. Perhaps Fort thought it was wiser to pretend that he didn't know, and keep on living."

"If I could get the chance, I'd like to argue with Tiffany about a few things. I'd like to point out that Fort recommended 'temporary acceptance' of all things. They seem to be adopting the attitude of 'automatic rejection'. Outright rejection of any claim, unless you can support it with logical reasons, is dogmatic. They're in danger of getting to the point where they'll be guilty of the very thing they are supposed to be fighting, namely: Rejecting all data which does not conform to their preconceptions. I'm just a dumb little ray-ro, not an intellectual writer in an ivory tower, but, from here, it seems to me that Tiffany and the other high priests of the Fortean religion ought to sort of count themselves."

"I'm not opposed to Fort, or the Fortean Society. They have done a lot of good. I'd like to see it keep in shape where it can keep on doing a lot of good. But that means that it can't stand still. Any thing that stops advancing decays and dies. They ought to let their minds un-jell, and let a new idea in now and then. Until they do, 'Thou shalt not mention the Caverns!' They aren't sactified by 'The Books.'"

"Good bye now. There will be convoys coming back from time to time for food, if they can get thru. We'll contact you then, if we can. They won't be coming back very often, and whether or not we can 'talk' when we do come back depends on the circumstances. I'll be seeing you again sometime, I hope."

* * * * * * *

MANDARK

By RICHARD S. SHAVER

Concluding the tremendous 200,000 word Novel

- - - the true story of the Life of Christ

Derek was not able to tell whether the knife was penetrating or not - for the struggling, terrible strength of the ape was too much for him. Suddenly the fingers of the ape found a hold upon the arm around his neck, and the ape swung forward in a bend, flung Derek head over heels to the ground in front of him. Derek struck in a roll and end over ended to his feet just in time to evade the follow-up charge of the ape, repeat his former tactic which had seemed to work as anything was going to work, got a good choking hold on the heavy hairy throat, raked across his belly with the knife. Suddenly the great white ape col'apsed like a bag of wind. Derek found himself suddenly the center of a shout of applause from the crowd. He looked around, but the other apes paid little attention to him, snuffled about, made no moves to attack. Derek walked slowly back toward the wooden door by which he had entered. As he approached, it swung wide, let him in. The apes were now driven out of the arena, his part was played.

Blaine wrung his hand. "Lucky strike, eh? I thought sure the thing would kill you, never saw one killed with a knife before. But it's evident you don't rattle easily. Pretty cool customer. If I live, I've got something to talk over with you."

- - - - -

There is little use going over the bloody account of the days waste of life in that arena under Jerusalem - there are a number of such accounts in writers who purvey blood and thunder exclusively - we have another purpose in this story, and it is not describing Tarzan meetings with the hairy lords of the Jungles or of the caverns either. The white apes are natives of certain garden areas of the caverns where the ancient lights have been kept in repair and the ancient art of gardening underground by these lights, much as a greenhouse is kept in the arctic circle - as they are-and as such they are only interesting in that they show the awful endurance the Elder race built into every bit of the apparatus they equipped the caverns with - the wonder of their life in caverns where no sun ever shines, the wonder of their gardens - as large as many surface governments - tier on tier of artificial brilliance and wild jungle growing now where once grew cultured plants set by the Gods themselves.

Most will not believe that such garden areas exist in the caverns, but they do so exist. But that is another story - I am writing to tell you of life that has survided the strange conditions of the caverns - the kind of men who are willing and able to keep the vast secret of their Elder world from us for all these silent centuries, the kind of life they lead - and what they mean to us. I am sorry it has to be done in a story form, but the story is entirely too unbelievable to be presented in any other way than lurid fiction - and still get a hearing. And a hearing I will have.

- - - - -

The bloody, stupid mess of the circus over, Derek and Blaine were returned to their former pens. Blaine was wounded, his arm sorely slashed by his opponent in a knife fight.

"He was an expert, I won by a trick - nearly got me - but I tripped him, and they put thumbs down on him. Just like Rome, eh - makes you feel like you're in the movies."

"Yeh, I felt like I was in the movies - mother naked they shove me out there and all those girls looking and laughing at me. How come you got clothes and I aint?"

"Look Derek, nothing is consistent and sane, the way we expect it. They don't think that way - everything is like the Mad Hatter's Tea Party down here - no rhyme or reasons, and that is a hard thing to learn. We are brought up to expect certain reactions, certain thoughts are standard in the kind of people we were brought up with. Down here that isn't true. These people are the produce of an entirely different kind of life - and nothing is orderly like we expect - nothing sane and thoughtful about it. So don't expect it. Expect the worst, and you might be surprised but the chances are you wont."

"Yeh, I know, Anything can happen. But nothing will except what you don't want."

"Look, Verne, if we make it happen, something might come right for us. I think we might have a chance."

"What the heck could we do. I can't figure how to take hold of a thing like this, they got everything. We aint even got a weapon, they got weapons that could defeat the U. S. Army - we don't even have a knife. How do you figure we can do anything about anything. Why even now a ray must be listening to us."

Even as Derek spoke, an invisible hand brushed his shoulder, a sweet voice in his ear said -"We do not all love this life. Most of the tyrants bunch are dead drunk now. Suppose you had help, are you willing to die for your wish to be free?"

"Hell we'll die anyway" - swore Blaine - "Lead on."

"The door of your cage has not been locked - did you notice? They are used to trusting the ever present ray to catch attempted escapists and bring them back - they do not always lock the door - it seems so unnecessary.

Go, and follow where I lead. Swiftly and talk to no one. I will explain if any ask questions."

Without question, Blaine and Derek walked out the door closing it behind, the shadows were deep, no one would miss them immediately. Down the deserted corridors of ancient stone they sped, walking fast - the occasional guard who paid no attention - they were so used to obeying a ray - having a ray scornfully assure them they were of no use that it never occurred to them anything could happen that was not supervised by an invisible ray. There was no invisible ray lashing whip-like at their shoulders, but hos could the guard know that. There was a ray gently guiding them by almost imperceptible pressures right and left through the maze of passages up, down, across and aback. They could never find their way back and there was no reason to come back.

Now they began to meet other people, all going the same direction and all of whom either ignored them or winked slightly at them, remembering they were warriors who had lived through the afternoon's bloody entertainment.

Now they entered a great chamber, nearly dark - and nearly full of people - squatting quietyly in rows, or reclining at length. As they came in there was a flurry of awakening attention near the far end of the room, and a slight girlishfigure leaped upon a great God-chair (a seat some eight to twenty times the size of a normal adult chair as we know it - the Gods were of various sizes - none small - according to their age) and began to speak. She spoke in American, then paused while a dark little man beside her made a swift translation in Arabic. Derek was noticing the Arabic faces mixedwith some American and strangely, there was little difference, a slightly more olive complexion - both were lighter than normal surface men - a sharper, more beaked nose - the differences ceased there.

"Friends, for four years we have suffered the vilest form of slavery. Our numbers have steadily decreased under the murderous rule of this Roden Harle - the madman from the north Hudson country - from Table Basen. We have no choice, we must either kill him soon or their will be none of us left to try to kill him. Tonight we have chosen, after terribly difficult preparation. The inner clique are all drunk tonight after the slaughter in the arena - we have no time for words - you all hate him and know you will die or live in the greatest degradation - in misery till you do die. We are going to go there, the ray who are with us have prepared the way - it is but for us left to take weapons and go in to the machine of life and kill all the old immortal devils that are left there in the insulated portions unreachable by the ray. They are in deadly danger until we succeed in penetrating into the metal rooms of the ancient Yahveh - the black Messiah, where they hide out - where they lie drunk in their debauchery, waiting for the knife - or where they wait to kill us - to trap us, and then spring to the vast weapons of the ancient last God, Yahveh and slay us all - no one knows - we can but try. Go quiety, stealthily, and if any ask questions, lie carefully for all of us live now but by the merest chance. Luck go with you, if we fail we all die; if we win, we all may live such a life as you know is possible to live with these mighty God machines to help us live happily - Go!

At the door as we passed out a little grey creature - an old woman, handed each of us a weapon from a pile. Derek received a short little tube, some eight inches long by an inch and a half in dia. He looked at it, puzzled. The old woman smiled a toothless, rather grim smile and said -"Press the button, but point it first - people will die for you quickly, but you will wonder where they have gone after they die - it is a potent weapon - go use fast, find man from people I love."

Something of nobility and courage passed into Derek from the toothless old woman who looked like but little, but as their hands touched Derek received a vital charge of energy from her body - an impulse saying - "Remember, we have been your guardian angles for centuries. We love you now as we have always done - fight for us as we have fought for you in the past - remember there are white witches as well Back" and Derek looked for the voice - the strength, and the old woman only smiled her toothless grin and pushed him gently with her hand. Derek realized he had merely experienced a slight sample of the thing men call magic. After all Derek realized - these are the people who have always worked the magic of the world and they should know a little about it.

Through the doors of the life machine as Derek called it, though he noticed that a great name over the door proclaimed it to be the "Satantes Dom" whatever that was. The home of some mighty Titan of the past.

HOUSE FOR SALE ON LILY LAKE

SEVEN ROOM SWISS CHALET TYPE DWELLING

This beautiful home now available. Contains three bed-
rooms, living room, knotty pine dining room, full bath
with linen closet, glazed sun-porch, modern kitchen and
basement garage with full basement. Oil heat furnace
in cellar, hot and cold running water. Land consists
of four lots beautifully landscaped, situated facing
Lily Lake and separated from all other property by
gravel roads. Fenced in yard. With the property
goes lake rights and a boat, one year old.

                        Address inquiries to Box 68,
Route 2, McHenry, Illinois.

In they marched, by twos and by threes and by singles all with
weapons concealed in their clothing, all afraid - all going ahead
into that fear, none speaking, walking with the same hopeless, joy-
less step that had marked their every day for years.

Inside, all was much the same, except that no ray lashed at them
with harsh words from some unseen distance. Something had happened
to them - and Derek guessed what it might have been.

Derek pushed straight ahead, hoping to find the black hearted fool
who had slain the girl on the target where had had last seen him.
He held on the tube before him, and as he entered the room of the
target, he heared laughter, the deeper toned chortle of a man, the
light giggle of a silly woman following. No one was in sight, and
Derek pushed ahead quietly, looking for a door that must be ajar
to hear the laughter - behind it he could hear the quiet feet of
man pushing cautiously through the place, hoping to cover the whole
before they were discovered. As Derek reached the low arched door
into the small chamber, saw on the bed the two bodies, the drunken
disorder of the whole room, felt the terrible augmentation of the
stim pleasure impulses from the glowing apparatus beside the bed,
realized the trance of sex which the machine had imposed upon the
two, he knew he had his bird. Noting a line of sighting projection
along the tube, he raised it to his eye, centered the thing carefully
on the prone man, whose face was turned toward his companion, on the
far side of the couch -

The rage he had felt that first day when he had seen the man murder
a woman for pleasure swept over Derek in a made flood as he pressed
the strange button on the unfamiliar, antique weapon, praying it
was what the old woman had assured him it was - a potent weapon.
Even as he pressed, the cylinder in his hand hummed, the recoil
snapped the thing back in his hand, and the place where the ruler,
Roden Harle, lay with his concubine, disappeared in a clud of grey
dust. The whole lounge had disappeared, the silken covers lay in
charred fragments on the floor - everything was gone. There was
only a large black hole in the polished stone of the floor - and
as Derek gazed into that dark hole, and saw it stretched down and
down and down, he knew what that shafthe had followed into his
place had once been - the discharge of some such weapon as this
and no work at all in its building. He stood there a long time
before the awe of their handiwork left him, and his mind returned
from the past that had been the life of the Elder race, to this
made scramble that was going around him for the power of the ancient machine - the home of past might that decided who ruled the
caverns of Onderde, as Derek knew now they were called.

Even as he turned from the wonder of the hole that had appeared
where the hated Roden Harle had lain, he heared racing footsteps
behind and the girl who had given them the sendoff talk in the
lower chambers rushed into the room, her hand holding a long
shinging wand, the tip glowing a deadly red. She exclaimed sharply
- "Oh, you've killed him outright. We had planned on giving him a
little time to think upon his sins - you have robbed us of our
pleasure."

Derek gazed at the savage, shining face of the girl, the blood that
rushed so vengefully through her cheeks, and put his hand on her
arm.

"You are right, he should have died more slowly, but I did not
think - I did not care to have him live one moment longer than was
necessary - it is better he is dead and out of the way. Now show
me every room in this place so that we know that nowhere is this
rat's nest does any living thing lurk that can ever harm you or

yours, or me or mine again. And then we must swiftly make sure
that only sane good men and women are appointed to power, we must
have an election, so that all will have a choice in saying who is
to rule. We must make sure that an honest way of life goes on
here after this - something like the elections of the surface
people of the United States."

"Come, you are right, even now, someone worse may be reaching for
the levers of the master ray - and we must be there to see it is
the right man and not the wrong one. Come, you are the one who
fought the ape, I remember you, you were fine - you come on" - and
she raced off, her hair flying, her feet nimble ahead and Derek
raced after, her excitement kindling him now, and the prospect for
real final success kindling - the dead feeling out of his heart -

The girl called back over her shoolder - "First one there at the
master beam will be the "Boss" til we held an election.

Derek Verne remained in the caverns. He remained in the great
machine that prolonged life and made of it something near the
fabled Nirvana of the eastern religious myths. He remained as one
of the council of seven who rule now those caverns where Yahveh
had suffered and lost his birthright of wisdome to the evil Lila
Onderde. Mahap his work in the future will make up for the loss
to men of such as Yahveh in the past.

For now, today, in the caverns in many places labor and study men,
modern men from the surface states. The old lore is being made
once again a part of the mind of man, and in the hope for the future
when death recedes into a minor place in life - when age has become
a thing of the past, the hope for a God Like race of man is growing
apace.

Let us hope that many such men as Derek Verne reach the caverns and
attain to a knowledge of the ancient science.

THE

END

OF

"M A N D A R K "

(In future issues will be some added commentary and
needed explanatory matter.)

Next issue beings another serial tale - perhaps by
Shaver, perhaps by some other, but - it will be about
the Elder caverns.)